TRUST

RILEY EDWARDS

TRUST

RILEY EDWARDS

Image/art disclaimer: Licensed material is being used for illustrative purposes only. Any person depicted in the licensed material is a model.

Editor: Cindy Wolken

Proofreader: Deaton Author Services

Cover Artist: Riley Edwards

Interior Design/Formatting: Riley Edwards

Published in the United States of America

Riley Edwards

This is a work of fiction. While reference might be made to actual historical events or existing locations, the names, characters,

ISBN: 978-1-7339667-5-7

This book is dedicated to our first responders. Those brave men and women who put their lives on the line each and every day. And to the families who stand behind these heroes and support them. Thank you! We are forever in your debt.

"There is a sacredness in tears. They are not the mark of weakness, but of power. They speak more eloquently than ten thousand tongues. They are the messengers of overwhelming grief, of deep contrition, and of unspeakable love."
~Washington Irving

PROLOGUE

New York, Hudson Federal Penitentiary

"The streets of the Sea Cliff area of San Francisco are beginning to look like a war zone as the National Guard has been called in. Another mob of angry citizens has gathered in support of the protesters who have surrounded City Hall and the Northern District Police Station where Channel 9 News is told Police Chief Brown is in the building with his detail.

"However, he's refused to comment on what began as a peaceful candlelight vigil for nine-year-old Holly Springs. The little girl was gunned down during what is being called a gang turf war..." I tuned the reporter's high-pitched voice out as she continued to blather on. The fucking bitch had no sense of self-preservation. She stood on the sidewalk trying to get her story as people threw trash cans and other objects at store windows and cars.

I never did understand why people destroyed their own neighborhoods when they were angry. Outsiders liked to look at me in disgust and revulsion. They called me a monster—a criminal. It's because of people like me there's order on the streets. We live by a code—a set of rules. When those rules are broken... we handle it.

In-house.

We don't waste taxpayers' money on an expensive trial through the justice system. We take care of our own. When you're guilty, you get what you deserve—a five-cent execution. Hell, sometimes it's even free if I want to get creative and get my hands dirty.

But these fuckin' *babbos* on the street aren't doing shit but making a mess.

I continue to watch the bitch on the TV make an ass out of herself as she runs into the street to shove her microphone in someone's face. I'll tell you what, if she shoved that thing in my face—I'd shove it up her ass.

Speaking of ass, a blonde with a smokin' ass encased in a pair of jeans came on to the screen, and my unused cock jerked to life.

The blonde turned, stepping into the street showing her face, and I was out of the hard metal chair, my cock deflated and forgotten. I was on my feet walking to the TV for a closer look.

It was her.

My gut recoiled at the sight of her. She was a blonde now, her natural brown hair bleached, but there was no hiding her identity.

Harper Russo.

I had waited years for this day and I finally found her.

"Guard," I called. "I need to use the phone."

Gotcha, bitch.

DONE

Mac

"Detective Aiden Mackenzie?" an older woman with shoulder length salt and pepper hair stopped me as I rushed past my desk in an effort to leave the station. She looked vaguely familiar, but in my rush, I couldn't place her. My mind was too preoccupied. A certain frustrating female had taken up all of my mental energy at the moment.

"Yes. May I help you?" I asked, coming to a stop in front of her.

"I'm sorry to bother you, Detective Mackenzie, especially with all those people gathered outside. The desk clerk said I could wait for you here."

"Mac, please," I offered, hoping this wasn't going to take long. A call had just come through that there was a group of protesters in Sea Cliff near Del Mar's. Laura had worked the morning shift and wasn't answering her cell, not that it was all that unusual for her. Recently she had been answering my calls less and less. And if I was honest, I was beyond annoyed.

In the nine months we'd been together, instead of getting closer, she had built more goddamned walls and pulled away. Not that she'd ever been open with me about her feelings, or *any-fucking-thing*. However, in the last few weeks, she'd patched and reinforced the tiny cracks I'd been able to make.

Yeah, I was pissed. In the middle of what was quickly becoming a citywide riot, she wasn't answering her goddamn cell phone. I had half a mind to text her and tell her I would be bending her over my knee this evening and paddling her ass raw. She needed a reminder of who was in control. That was part of why we'd started this journey. Control. Her need to lose it, and my need to take it. When I saw her in Stripes, a local BDSM club, I was both ecstatic to find out she had similar tastes as I did, and furious she was there alone. That night I sat at the bar nursing my Jack and Coke, watching her from a distance. She didn't know I was lurking only a few feet away; she had no clue I was studying her every move. I waited to approach her until she was about to leave, purse in hand, and headed for the door. The shocked look on her face when she saw me, and her stuttered excuses about why she was there, were comical.

It took me all of thirty minutes to lay out the ground rules, and go over limits, before I had her bent over the spanking bench. Fast? Maybe. Necessary? Absolutely. If I'd allowed her to walk out of Stripes, she would never have summoned up the courage to come back. It was very obvious from my observation that she needed to be there. After a month of playing in the main public areas of the club, I finally took her into a private room. Another month after that before I played with her outside of the club. She was new to domination, bondage, toys, and discipline. For the first three months of our D/s contract, I was painstakingly slow in my exertion of power, only giving her more when those beautiful amber eyes of hers lit up in wonderment. This was about the journey after all, and I wanted her to enjoy every second of it.

Now, during a scene seemed to be the only time I felt close to her; when she let go and allowed me to take care of her. Wasn't that a bitch? I needed to remind Laura that we had a D/s contract in place every time I wanted to hold her after we had sex. That as her Dom, I made the rules, and that included if I wanted to cuddle and gently caress her after sex.

The woman was maddening.

Commotion in the room brought me back to the present, reminding me I needed to get to Del Mar's before the protesters turned violent. The mayor called in the National Guard to help keep the peace after an irresponsible reporter escalated the already volatile situation when she cited an unnamed source that said the police chief was on the take and not doing everything he could about the gang violence that had started to spread over the I-80 into the San Francisco area from Oakland. The PC was a dick and rumors had been circulating for a long time that he had been accepting bribes from a local mob family. However, no one had gotten close enough to get actual proof. Mostly because cops wanted to keep their jobs.

"Thank you. I know this sounds so silly, but I was told that you were the detective that was working burglaries in the North Beach area?"

Yes. That's where I knew her from. She was one of the homeowners. "Yes. Mrs. Sinclair, correct?" I asked.

"Yes, that's me. I was told that the man behind the break-ins had been arrested. I know this is a long shot but has any of the jewelry been recovered?"

"Yes, Ma'am, we did. But only a few pieces were found. We're still hoping he'll give up his partner, and we'll recover more of the stolen property. Did you list all of the items that were taken?"

"Indeed," she answered and then crestfallen, she mumbled, "Thank you for your time." She turned to leave, the tears in her eyes a kick to my gut.

"Was something special taken?" I don't know why I asked. It didn't matter if it was special or not, the woman's home was entered without her permission. Her possessions taken, the value didn't matter, yet I felt compelled to ask.

"A locket my husband gave me when we were teenagers." She wiped the tear from the corner of her eye. "It was for my fifteenth birthday."

"Maybe you can describe it to me," I offered and rummaged through the files on my desk until I found the case I was looking for. As desperate as I was to get to Laura, I couldn't in good conscience let this woman leave until I at least gave her an answer.

"It's a tiny gold heart. It doesn't look like much, but it means the world to me."

I thumbed through the photographs we'd processed into evidence and stopped on an image of an old and tarnished locket.

"Is this it?" I turned the glossy eight by ten image her way, and the sweetest smile spread across her wrinkled face.

"Yes. That's it, my locket," she gasped.

I turned the picture over and scribbled her name

on the back, thankful I could give this woman a measure of relief.

"It normally takes about ten days for us to process out evidence. When the necklace is ready to be picked up, I'll call you."

"Thank you so much, Detective Mackenzie. You'll never understand what you gave me back."

"Glad it was found. Come on, I'll walk you out to your car. I've heard it is getting rowdy out there."

While I walked Mrs. Sinclair to her car, she explained that locket was one of the few pieces of jewelry her husband had given her. They had five children and money was always tight. It was more important to them that their family was taken care of than frivolous gifts. My heart broke for the old woman as she told me how the thought of losing something so special had been devastating. I navigated us through the throngs of people outside of the station and safely put her in her car with the promise I would call her soon.

There was something in the way Mrs. Sinclair spoke of her locket that reminded me of Laura, and how she spoke of her grandmother's scarlet emerald necklace. I thought back to the day I found it on Laura's nightstand. In one declaration, she told me it was nothing, and in the next, she claimed it was her most valued possession. I hadn't seen the necklace since and that was months ago. That small tidbit of information was the most she'd ever opened up about. I still knew nothing about Laura's past. Being a detective, I could've run a background check. However, doing so seemed to be crossing a line I didn't want to cross. Besides, I wanted her to trust me enough to tell me her story. What had happened to her that made her so skittish? Who hurt her so deeply that she hid behind a façade of indifference? There was so much to Laura; she was a walking contradiction. Hard and soft. Nonchalant and passionate.

I took in the disorderly crowd gathering around the station and shook my head. I was pleased as fuck I was no longer in uniform and didn't have to stand guard outside the precinct during times of unrest. My temper was too short for that bullshit.

Once I'd driven a few blocks, the mob thinned and the streets were normal. Personally, I thought the mayor was overreacting calling in the National Guard, but he was known for being extremely oversensitive and famous for making rash decisions. Thirty minutes later, I was pulling into Del Mar's. A few people were milling about but it looked like whatever crowd had gathered had been quickly dispersed by the police.

I parked in the lot behind the café and made my way to the front entrance.

"What the hell?" I asked when I found my friend,

Reid, out front with a push broom sweeping up glass from the sidewalk.

"Trash can through the front window," he clipped, his tone low and close to a growl. "Stupid fucks."

"Ava?" I asked about his wife. "Laura?"

"Inside. Laura's fine. Ava's taking it pretty hard. Just because Del Mar's has been officially sold to Suzie and Michael, doesn't mean that Ava still doesn't love this place. She's heartbroken."

Ava had opened Del Mar's after Jacob, her first husband, was killed in the line of duty. She had only recently sold it to Suzie and her husband Michael, who was a fellow cop. Ava had decided she wanted to stay home with JJ and Melody, her and Reid's children. I was happy Ava had finally found the peace and happiness she deserved.

I looked through the now glassless window frame and saw Laura, Ava, and Suzie were sitting at the counter. The normally bustling café almost empty. Laura had a towel wrapped around her hand, the blood easily seen even from where I stood. Without thinking about the audience we had, I stormed the café, stopping beside her.

"What the hell happened?" I demanded, harsher than I should've if the narrowing of Laura's eyes were any indication.

"Nothing. It's just a little cut." Her eyes slid down and to the right, a clear sign she was lying.

I was fed up with keeping our relationship a secret. Her demand, not mine, and one that I had respected for months.

I was done.

2

MY BOYFRIEND

Laura

I saw it, the moment it happened. In the space between my carefully constructed life being blown to hell, there was a shift in Mac. I had known it was only a matter of time. I was stupid believing I could keep our secret this long. My time was up—it had been up for a long time. I knew better than to get close to anyone, especially the pragmatic detective. I had even allowed myself to form a friendship with Ava. That might have been the nail in my coffin. The final straw that was going to be my downfall.

"Laura," Mac growled, and I fought the urge to drop to my knees in front of him. "I'm taking you home."

Ava's head swiveled to Mac, and she glared at him. "She's fine, Mac. We cleaned it off and wrapped it," she explained. My sweet friend was trying to defuse the situation.

"Is that why it's bleeding through the towel?" he returned.

Reid strolled in looking like he was ready to strangle the person who dared to vandalize Ava's beloved café. It didn't matter that ownership had been transferred to Suzie days before, making her my new boss. Ava had often said that the café was the only thing that kept her sane during a time of great sadness, that and her son JJ. Now she had Reid and his daughter, Melody, too. I was glad that she was settling into her life with them. They had a family, and Ava deserved to be happy.

"Does that need stitches?" Reid asked, motioning toward my bloody hand.

Great.

"No. I'm fine. I'll clean it up when I get home."

I tried to stand and beat feet before Mac could say any more, but his large frame stood unmoving. "We're going to the ER," Mac announced.

My heart began to thunder in my chest and panic rose to the surface. "That's... not necessary," I stammered.

There was no way I could go to the ER. I hated hospitals. I had spent weeks lying in a hospital bed under police protection while I recovered from the worst beating of my life. Falling into a drug-induced sleep every night, afraid they would find me and finish the job and I'd never wake up. The first few days after surgery, I'd wished that I'd never been found. Dying on the cement floor of a dingy warehouse would've been better than what my life had turned into. I had nothing.

One man, my own blood, had destroyed everything.

Mac looked down at me, his features softening, and when his hand came to my face, his thumb gently grazing my skin, I melted. For a moment, I'd forgotten we were in public; and when I looked into his blue eyes, they held me captive, and my body relaxed. I would take this small comfort from him. Something I usually never allowed.

Reid cleared his throat, drawing me back to the present. I tried to step back, but Mac pulled me closer to him, wrapping both his arms around me, trapping mine between our bodies.

"No more, Laura. Playtime's over. For nine months, we've done it your way. I see that was a mistake. I thought I was giving you time to come to trust me. For you to work through whatever nasty shit is swirling around in your head." My body stiffened at his words. "No more lies."

My time was officially up. I had planned on leaving

first thing tomorrow morning but tonight seemed like a better option.

Yet another reason I hated Frankie Russo. I had to let Mac go.

Someone nearby cleared their throat followed by, "Laura?" The familiar voice shocking me more than Mac's declaration.

Quinn Alexander.

I turned in Mac's arms, breaking our connection to face my old friend. If that's what you could call Quinn. Sadly, the US Marshal was the closest thing I had to an actual comrade. His face was unreadable as he stood in the doorway of the café. Once upon a time, he was supposed to walk me through the lonely steps of entering into the Witness Protection program. When I declined at the last minute, Quinn tried his best to talk me into going. However, I couldn't bring myself to become Betty Appleton from *nowheresville*, Iowa. Instead, I became a string of aliases there were so many names over the years I couldn't remember them all. Funny that the one name I wanted to forget, my birth name, I couldn't.

It didn't matter how far I ran or for how long. I would always be Harper Russo of the Russo Crime Family. I would forever be labeled a rat. It didn't matter that I didn't believe in the code or hold any value in the *Omerta*. I was born into a screwed-up family with a broken moral compass.

"A word?" Quinn asked.

Wait. What was Quinn doing in San Francisco? Last I spoke to him he was living down in San Diego.

Mac straightened and started to move me behind him. "And you are?" Mac asked.

I studied Quinn and made a split-second decision. This was my chance to make a clean break. I hated to use him to do it, but I had no other choice. I had to make Mac hate me so much he'd never come looking for me. Quinn was a good-looking man. Tall, lean, tanned skin—made more so by the Southern California sun, muscular enough I could see some definition under the polo shirt he wore.

"My boyfriend," I blurted out. Quinn's eyes widened in shock before he quickly recovered, masking his surprise.

I felt Mac's body recoil, and I wanted to pull the words back in. It was too late, I had started the course, and it really was for the best. Quinn Alexander once again was my saving grace.

"The fuck you say?" Mac's eyes pinned me in place. "Your boyfriend?" he spat out in disgust. "You've been in my bed for the past nine months, and you have a man?" Well, now everyone knew that Mac and I had been together. Actually, it was better they did; they could all hate me for breaking his heart. It would make my departure easier. They could all commiserate over my betrayal. Only it wasn't infidelity I was guilty of.

Mac's angry words pierced through the tough layer of scar tissue that had encapsulated my heart. This was for the best, I had to remind myself when the pain threatened to make me blurt out the truth. Perfect timing actually; now I had no choice but to leave. With each day that had passed, Mac was breaking down the barriers I'd built. Walls that were necessary for my survival.

"It's... um. We have an open relationship. And I never made you any promises. The thing between us was nothing more than fun," I lied. It was more—way more.

Mac locked eyes with Quinn, nodded, and moved to the double swinging doors that led to the back of the café. "Good to know," he muttered as the doors slammed open with such a force I was surprised they didn't break.

"Ready?" I asked Quinn, trying to make a quick exit.

And in my biggest bitch move to date, my biggest regret, I turned to Ava, Reid, and Suzie and waved goodbye. No words of apology, no explanation as to why I had ripped their friend's heart out. I didn't thank Ava for taking a chance and hiring me. I didn't thank her for her friendship and support. But more than all of that, I never told Mac how much I loved him, that in another place and time, I would've never left him.

Instead, I smiled and waved like it was no big deal and I would see them all again tomorrow. When I turned to walk to Quinn, I knew damn good and well that I would never step back into Del Mar's and I would never clap eyes on any of them again.

With one last look, I committed the café to memory. Of all the places I had been, this was my favorite. Quinn let the door close behind us, and it was then I allowed the first tear to fall.

3

NO MORE LIES...

Mac

I'd spent all day yesterday at the gym beating the shit out of a heavy bag trying to burn off my anger. It hadn't worked. How the fuck had Laura conned me? What sign had I missed? I had gone over our relationship trying to remember something, some clue she had given me, some doubt I had. There was nothing. Other than she never wanted to share her past with me. That should've been enough, but it wasn't. How the hell had she had a man all this time, and I didn't know it?

Now I was sitting at my desk, neck deep in a missing persons case, and something wasn't adding up. News broke that Nicole Brown, daughter of Police Chief Tom Brown, was missing. How had all the local media outlets caught wind of her supposed kidnapping before the chief himself briefed his department? It had been less than twenty-four hours, and the chief was sketchy on the details, only saying Nicole was at a candlelight vigil for Holly Springs, a little girl that had been killed in a gang turf war, and he hadn't spoken to her since.

Even though the chief named me the lead detective on the case, he hadn't disclosed how he knew his daughter was *missing*. How, after such a short amount of time, he *knew* she had been kidnapped. He had been adamant about it when he paced his office and threw his coffee cup across the room, shattering it when it collided with the drywall. He also flat out refused to entertain the idea there was a leak in his personal detail. However, someone had given a detailed report to the news channels. The man was distraught and frantic. Almost too much. There was a little too much terror in his voice. Nicole was an adult, she didn't live with him, and according to the police chief, there had been no call for ransom.

So how was it that Tom Brown *knew* without a shadow of a doubt his daughter was not only kidnapped but was in *grave* danger? Those had been his words. It didn't take a rocket scientist to figure out something wasn't adding up.

When I had asked chief why he wanted me on the case when I already had stacks of cases on my desk, he spouted off some bullshit reason about me being the best detective he had. I knew that was an excuse; he wanted me to use my connection to Logan Reid. And everybody knew Reid's reputation as a private investigator. He was the best there was. He also knew that I didn't have an issue with getting my hands a little dirty when I needed, skirting the line of the law as close as one can without going over.

Nicole was last seen dropping her dachshund puppy off at Woofle Waffle Play Days. The trendy doggy daycare had just opened not too long ago but had quickly caught on. The manager, Hisoka Tsukuda, had already checked out with a strong alibi. I had yet to question any of her friends or search her apartment. My gut was telling me that something wasn't right. Nicole was well liked, not apt to party or drink. No string of boyfriends. She was an all-around nice young girl. The exact opposite of her father.

I grabbed my cell and pocketed it before picking up my coffee. I wasn't going to find the information I needed doing internet searches. Her social media accounts had already turned up nothing. I needed to interview witnesses. I stopped short when the guy from the café, Laura's boyfriend, was walking toward me.

"You got a minute?" he asked.

His short-cropped brown hair was disheveled like someone had been running their hands through it. Probably Laura. Anger started to rise to the surface, thinking about the two of them in bed together. Him being the man that Laura shared her life with, leaving me to be the man she only *fucked*. I got no other part of her—he got it all.

"Nope. I'm on a case. And don't bother coming back because I don't have a goddamn thing to say to you."

I started to walk around him. I had shit to do and sitting down to file a mountain of paperwork after I beat the fuck out of him was not on today's agenda.

"She's gone," he announced.

"Who the fuck are you talking about?" I asked.

"Laura. She took off," he told me.

"And? Man, that's not my business. Don't bother me with your domestic issues."

He had some brass balls coming into my precinct to tell me Laura had left him. As if I'd give a shit.

"Is there someplace we can talk in private?" He stepped in front of me and brought his hand up, blocking my exit.

"I have someplace I have to be," I semi-repeated. "Now get the hell out of my way."

"She didn't tell you, did she?"

I didn't want to discuss with this man what Laura hadn't told me. The last thing I needed was to know how much she *had* told him.

"Who are you?" I finally asked the question I'd

been avoiding. I didn't want to put a name to the man that the woman I loved belonged to. "And how the hell did you get back here without an escort?"

"Deputy Quinn Alexander, US Marshal," he answered, pulling back his sport coat to flash his shield.

I cocked my head to the side and gave Quinn Alexander a once-over, from his khaki pants, neatly pressed crisp shirt, and stylish sport coat. He was awfully well dressed and not in an expensive name brand sort of way, more in a—he had a personal shopper way. Well, it seemed that Laura certainly had a type—a deputy and a detective.

"Come again?"

"Can you dial your jealousy down a few notches for five damn minutes? We need to talk in private," Quinn demanded, his tone becoming more urgent. "Now."

I relented.

Call it morbid curiosity, but now I was more interested than I should've been about what the man had to say.

"This way." I motioned for him to follow me to an empty interrogation room and shut the door.

"What can I do for you, *deputy*?" I asked, walking to the other side of the table. In my current mood, it was probably best for me to keep a safe distance.

"When was the last time you saw Laura?" he inquired.

"At the cafe," I spit out. "Right before she left with you."

Quinn studied me from across the table for a moment before he continued, "What did she tell you about her past?"

"I'm not real fond of being interrogated. Why don't you cut to the chase? If you're asking me if I know where your woman is—I don't. She never was good at answering her phone when I called. Guess I now know why."

"She loves you," Quinn started, putting up his hand to stop me when I started to protest. "She lied to you the other day. I am not her boyfriend. Not by a long shot. She's not my type, so to speak." Quinn chuckled. "I was in charge of getting her settled in WITSEC."

"What? WITSEC?" I questioned. There was no way he was talking about Laura.

"Witness Protection—"

"I know what the fucking program is," I cut him off. "Why would Laura be in WITSEC?"

Quinn was silent for long moments before he lifted his face to the heavens and on a long exhale he started. "I am only telling you this because I know she loves you, even if she won't admit it. And by the look of devastation on your face when she lied and said she was involved with me, I'd say you love her, too." I started to tell him to mind his own damn business when he put his hand out to stop me. "Don't bother denying it, because I really don't want to hear it. What I need is for you to shut up and listen. Her real name is Harper Russo. Ring any bells?"

My temper was flaring, and anger was bubbling to the surface. Who the hell did this guy think he was? The words *fuck you* were on the tip of my tongue when the name he said hit me. Harper Russo? Why did that name sound so familiar? Before I could come up with an answer, he continued.

"Her brother is Frankie Russo—of the Long Island, New York, Russos. He took over for his father after the old man was whacked at the family's pizzeria. Marco Russo was as close to a good-guy boss as you can find in the mob. Frankie? Exact opposite. All the things his father kept off the table, a stable of girls, human trafficking, high-interest loans, Frankie not only put them back on the table but demanded his soldiers deliver." Quinn stopped for a minute and sat in the metal chair, stretching his legs out in front of him. "Harper saw something she wasn't supposed to. Frankie was pissed, to put it mildly. They argued, but she wouldn't change her point of view on the situation, so Frankie did what he does best. He tried to physically convince her to see things his way."

"The scars on her legs," I mindlessly said, remembering all the times I had asked what the scars were from. Questions that Laura had refused to answer. Kissing each long line of raised skin up her otherwise flawless flesh. Her legs were beautiful.

"Yeah—nice fucking brother, huh? She held out as long as she could. Frankie left her on the floor of one of his warehouses. He thought he'd killed her and called in a soldier to dump her body somewhere and make it look like a rival did it. In an unusual act of humanity, the soldier dropped her off behind a police station and called 9-1-1 to report where he'd left her."

I felt like I was listening to the plot of some mafioso drama. Who the fuck did that to their own family? Somewhere in my musings, it hit me we were talking about Laura—not some unknown woman named Harper Russo.

"Where the fuck is she?" I shouted.

"Good, it's finally sinking in. It's about time. That's why I am here, Detective. Harper...Laura... was inadvertently caught on a news broadcast reporting the riots around the city. She was in the background crossing the street. She was on camera long enough for me to immediately recognize her. And if I recognized her, that means there's a possibility that one of

Frankie's guys did. They have a million reasons to be on the lookout for Harper. Frankie went all out this time—a cool mil to kill his sister. Or he himself could've seen her on TV. Who knows? It's not like he has much else to do sitting on his ass in the pen. However small the chance, it was still too big—I couldn't risk her life and assume no one else saw her. I needed to warn her, and she needed to leave the city immediately. That's why I went to Del Mar's. It was sheer coincidence I'd transferred to the area from San Diego a few months ago—not that I can't say I'm not thankful for the good luck."

"How did you know where she was if she had refused WITSEC?"

"Just because she refused doesn't mean I was going to throw her to the wolves. I trained her how to stay off grid and how to disappear if needed. Unfortunately, I may have taught her too well because I can't find her. I had an emergency call and had to leave her to pack up her stuff. I gave her the address to a safe house if she had to split. When I got back to her place about three hours later, it'd hadn't been ransacked. From the evidence at the scene, she got away, but someone knew where to find her in the first place. And she's not at the safe house, nor is she answering her phone. I had a contact try to track it, but it's turned off. With her not in the program, my hands are tied. If I fill out a missing persons report on her, that opens a whole new can of worms that can't be closed again." Pulling a business card out of the inside chest pocket of his sport coat, Quinn placed it on the table. "I read your file earlier before making the decision to come here. Commendations, medals, fast-tracked to detective—all and all, you look like a damn good cop. I hope that's not just on paper. I can't use my office to track Harper or use federal resources. Officially, your hands are as tied as mine, but I know you have connections in the city that I don't. Not up here, not yet. If we're going to find Harper before they do, I'll need you to call in some markers."

"There is no we in this. I don't know you." I moved to the door and stopped Quinn from speaking. "You said you just transferred up here, yeah?" Quinn nodded. "Don't you have a desk to unpack?"

I didn't know why I was still jealous of the man. He'd explained why Laura had lied, and it was very obvious that he had no interest in her other than professionally. I could understand how he'd come to care about Laura, but it was never a good idea to get emotionally involved with a witness or victim. However, there were times where you couldn't stop it. Much like with Mrs. Sinclair, I genuinely cared for the old woman. I assumed that was how Quinn felt about Laura.

Maybe I was resentful because he knew the real Laura Barnett. The woman, not the name. That's what was bothering me; he knew more about the woman I loved than I did.

Quinn's eyes narrowed as he stood from the chair. "I'm feeling rather generous this morning. I'll give you a pass on your bullshit, this once. I get she hurt you, and she used me to do it. Get the fuck over yourself, and hurry. Harper's out there alone with a bounty on her pretty, little head. Call me when you've figured out you need me more than you think you do."

Christ.

Nothing like having your ass handed to you before you've finished your first cup of coffee. Worst part? He was fucking right. I needed him.

4

____

SEVENTEEN

Laura

My teeth were chattering so hard I was surprised I hadn't chipped one. South Lake Tahoe was cold as balls and in my haste to run out the door, I hadn't grabbed my jacket. Quinn was going to be pissed I took off and hadn't checked in with him. There'd been no time. After he explained why he'd searched me out to speak in person, he took me back to my house so I could grab my stuff. I was supposed to meet up with him a few hours later. He was arranging a safe house and a meeting with a forger to get me new documents. Even though I had two sets, he was always over cautious making sure I had everything I needed. I appreciated his help; I needed it. But then, as I was finishing up there was a knock—yes, the assholes knocked on my door. I was about to answer it thinking it was Quinn when I heard a thick New York accent and snuck out the bedroom window and ran.

I had no idea how my brother had found me, or how he got his goons to California so quickly. Quinn said he'd only seen me on TV that day. We thought we had more time before I was in any real danger. I guess a million-dollar price tag made people move fast. I'd like to say it didn't matter *how* he found me, just that he *did*, but it mattered. My life depended on being one step ahead of the soldiers that were still loyal to my brother and the family. I had been so careful, other than staying in San Francisco longer than I normally stayed in one place. I knew better than to stay and make friends or fall in love with a man I had no business getting involved with.

Mac.

I was almost happy I had to ditch my phone before I'd boarded the bus to Reno. I spent the six-hour bus ride debating whether or not I should've called Mac and told him the truth. In the end, I decided I'd made the right choice. Better to have a broken heart than get dead. Frankie would never stop looking for me. I couldn't bring anyone into this. No one was safe when they were around me. I was a dead woman walking—stalked and hunted daily. It was only a matter of time before I slipped up and Frankie killed me. Sure, he wouldn't be the one pulling the trigger. He was serving a life sentence without parole in a federal penitentiary, however that didn't mean he still wasn't the boss. He was now safely tucked away where his enemies couldn't touch him, and he was free to conduct business without the fear of assassination.

Between the bus ride to Reno, Nevada, the hitchhiking with a trucker to Carson City, and hitching a ride with another truck driver back into California, I finally stopped in South Lake Tahoe. I was exhausted and chilled to the bone. I couldn't fly, couldn't rent a car, and couldn't book a decent hotel. I had no identification. On my way to the bus stop, I had thrown everything away in different dumpsters around San Fran. I couldn't take the chance that Frankie knew the last alias I had been using.

There I was lying on top of the itchy comforter in my nineteen-dollar-a-night motel too skeeved out to pull it back and lie on the sheets, contemplating my next move. I was so tired of living out of a backpack. Tired of having to be ready to move at a moment's notice. Tired of having to look over my shoulder every goddamn day. I wanted it to end. Sometimes I thought it would be easier to just let my brother find me and finally put me out of my misery. How much longer could I do this? Seventeen moves. Seventeen names. Seven-fucking-teen times having to start my life over from scratch. I owned nothing, had nothing, and would never have anything.

I hated my brother, despised everything my family stood for, and loathed the mafia. I'd lost everything because of the family I was born into. I tossed and turned the rest of the night feeling sorry for myself, wishing that I was back in my little guesthouse in San Francisco wrapped in Mac's arms. I had fought him every time he tried to cuddle with me, bristling at his gentle touches and soft kisses. But the truth was I desperately wanted them. I wanted to stay wrapped in him for the rest of my life.

By the time the sun was up, I was dressed and ready to hitch a ride to my next destination. I wish I could've gone someplace warm and sunny but the first thing that Quinn taught me was I had to do pretty much the opposite of what Harper Russo would've done. It was no secret I hated New York winters and complained the moment the temperature dropped below sixty degrees. My brother would expect me to hide where there was warm weather. Northern California had been the closest I had come to warmth since I started running. I had to call Quinn and see if he could get me a passport. I had never been able to afford one. A birth certificate, social security card, and driver's license were easy to find. A passport? That was big money, and I would need a really good forger to manage one that wouldn't get me arrested. It was time for me to leave the country. I was running out of places to hide—not only from my brother but from anyone I had met in the last few years. I couldn't begin to remember all the aliases I had used, or the people I had met.

After grabbing a cup of coffee at the truck stop in front of the hotel, I was still actively hating my life and mentally grumbling about having to once again run, when I realized that leaving a location had never hurt this bad. In the past, it had been annoying; an irritation that I had to upend my life. Never had it been cutting and painful. And it wasn't just Mac I missed, though that did hurt the most. I missed Ava, too. Why did I have to get involved? I had always been so careful not to get close to anyone.

I went in search of an ever-disappearing pay phone. With a pocketful of change, I dialed Quinn's number and waited for the recording to tell me how much money to deposit. Six rings later, it went to voice mail. Shit. He must've been neck deep in work if he wasn't answering. With my hand still on the receiver I stared at the phone. What could it hurt? Even if the call was somehow traced, I'd be long gone by the time someone got to Tahoe to look for me. I had already broken all the rules when it came to Mac. What was one more?

It was like a compulsion; I had to do it. I picked up the handset again, cradling it between my ear and my shoulder. With each push of a silver number I started to question why I was torturing myself. It wasn't like I was actually going to speak. I just wanted to hear his growly voice.

The phone rang, and my heart pounded in my chest, threatening to explode. "Mac," he greeted. I remained quiet, praying he would repeat his name so I could hear it one more time. Commit it to memory so I could recall it when I was lonely and ready to give up. "Hello?" he said again, "I can hear you breathing." I jumped and almost dropped the receiver. I quickly placed my hand over the mouthpiece. "I can help you," he said, lowering his voice. "Just tell me where you are, and I'll come get you." He must've thought I was someone else, maybe one of the victims he was working with. I felt guilty for a moment, but the feeling vanished as fast as it came. I needed this, I needed all the words I could get from him. "Laura, please." I hadn't meant to let out a whimper, but he heard. "I know everything. I can help."

He knew? There was no way; it was impossible.

"How?" I squeaked out.

"Trust me, baby, I can make you safe," he pleaded.

"You can't. No one can. Just forget me, Mac."

I pulled the phone away from my ear, getting ready

to hang up, but his words stopped me. "I'll never stop looking for you. I'll go to the ends of the earth to find you."

I didn't answer. There was nothing I could say to that. Unlike when my brother made the same promise, Mac's earnest vow filled me with warmth. Someplace deep inside I wished he would find me. I wished he could make this all go away.

5

DEAL WITH THE DEVIL

Mac

I knew what I'd find when I went to Laura's house yesterday, but I still had to go. I needed to see it for myself.

She was really gone.

With a knot in my gut I searched her almost empty house from top to bottom. I don't know what I was looking for, but I searched anyway. Quinn had filled me in enough that I could get the rest of the information on my own. Yet, I still combed over her home, searching for some clue as to where she would've gone. There was nothing. Quinn was right—he'd taught her well.

The kitchen, dining area, and living room all looked exactly like it had the last time I'd been there for dinner. It was hard to believe it was only days before we'd sat on her couch and watched a movie, ending the evening in her bed.

Her bedroom was the only room that had changed. She'd left in a hurry, not even bothering to empty out her drawers. The closet still had clothes hanging in it as well. A beautiful red gown hung in the back. I had never seen Laura wear anything other than casual clothes, but the dress was neatly preserved in a plastic garment bag. I spent hours at her house packing the rest of her clothes, shoes, and what few personal items she'd left behind. I would store them at my house until I found her. I'd finished loading the boxes into the back of my truck when, on an impulse, I pulled her sheets off the bed, deciding I wanted those, too. In my swiftness to yank the fitted sheet off the bed I moved the mattress and when I went to right it, I thanked all things holy that I had turned into a pussy and wanted to keep Laura's sheets because they smelled like her. Under her mattress was her grandmother's scarlet emerald necklace.

It was then the gravity of the situation hit me. How scared Laura must've been to run and not take the time to pack something that meant so much to her. I also realized I needed help; I couldn't find her on my own. But before I could reach out to Reid, I had to make a few calls. I didn't want to pull him into this anymore than I had to and put Ava and the kids in danger. Reid had a family now, and I wouldn't allow anything to screw that up.

It had taken me two phone calls and thirty minutes to find Nico Tuscani. Word on the street was that Nico was spending time in the Bay Area taking the necessary steps to rebuild the family name that Nico's father had all but ruined. With Nico's ties to New York I needed him, and I was about to make a deal with the devil. I had spent last night contemplating just how far I'd be willing go for Nico's help. There would be a hefty price–I was sure of it. No one asked for a favor from a Capo without knowing they were signing their soul over. By the end of the night I had resigned myself to the fact that the Tuscani family would own me. And I was okay with that if it meant that Harper Russo would be safe.

When I stepped into Nonna Maria's I waited, allowing my eyes to adjust to the low light of the little hole-in-the-wall restaurant. The deep maroons of the high back booths and traditional Italian décor transported me from downtown San Francisco to the streets of Sicily. I scanned the almost empty dining room and found Nico in the corner, his back to the wall, giving him the perfect view of the restaurant. He had one man that I could see with him, sitting to his left. They were both looking down, reading what looked like the newspaper from this distance.

Without waiting for the hostess, I moved toward the table and both men's gazes came up, assessing. The man with Nico stood, his hand going to the waistband of his slacks. I was in plain clothes, with my shield and gun on clear display. There was no reason to hide who I was.

"A word?" I asked Nico.

His eyes narrowed on me and without breaking contact he ordered, "Sit, Branson. I don't think the detective means me any harm." Nico chuckled, and Branson took his seat. "Aiden Mackenzie, what can I do for you?" Nico asked.

I didn't bother giving any thought to how the man knew my name. I suppose in his business it was paramount to know local law enforcement. As much as I wanted to get straight to it, I had to make a few things clear. "I'm not here on police business. I'd like to speak to you someplace private."

Nico continued to look at me. "If you're not here on official business, then why the fuck are you interrupting my lunch?"

If I didn't need this asshole so badly, I'd love nothing more than to tell him where he could shove his fucking lunch. "I want to talk to you about Frankie Russo."

I watched Nico closely as his nostrils flared the smallest fraction before he schooled his features once again, looking impassive. Perhaps I wouldn't owe quite so much for this favor; it seemed that Nico wasn't fond of little Frankie.

"What about him?"

I had Branson's attention, too. He had abandoned pretending to read the paper and was now giving me his full attention.

"What if I told you I had a few connections at the Hudson Federal Pen and I could make it real easy for one of your men to have a little chat with Frankie?"

Nico brought his napkin to his mouth and dabbed an invisible crumb off his lips before he set the napkin down and pushed his plate away. "I'd say I don't conduct business with law enforcement. Not to mention, I don't know a Frankie Russo. You must have me mistaken."

"Right. How 'bout this. You know Blaze, the President of Iron Claw MC? Call him and ask about me. After that conversation, if your memory say, gets jarred, and you remember who Frankie fucking Russo is—call me. I'm not interested in playing games. I walked in here today my shield on display as a show of respect. I have no interest in bullshitting you. If I don't get a call you have to know, I'll be extending this offer to one of your associates. It doesn't matter to me who disposes of the asshole, only that he is taken care of. But, I think it matters to you. After all, the Russos still control most of Nassau and Suffolk counties. If I'm not mistaken, that territory has been very profitable for many years. It'd be a shame if one of your competitors got their hands on it."

"You fucking threatening me?" Nico stood and faced me.

"Just stating facts. Blaze knows how to get ahold of me. There's a two-hour clock on this. After that, I'm making some calls."

I didn't wait for Nico's response. I didn't have time. I needed to talk to Reid and find Laura. Not to mention, Nicole Brown still hadn't shown up or called in. The chief was having a shit hemorrhage.

On the drive to Reid's, I contemplated how much I was going to tell him. By the time I was walking into his office I had decided on the whole truth. It was my best option.

Roni, Reid's pretty receptionist, was on the phone and waved me back to Reid's office. As I walked down the corridor leading to Reid's office, I stopped by a newly hung framed photograph. Most of the pictures in the hallway were of Reid's military friends. There was a plaque that hung above the frames that read, *Gone but not Forgotten*. The image that had garnered my attention was of Rick—a friend and one of Reid's employees. He had died trying to save Ava and JJ from a crazy stalker hell bent on taking her. The weight of the guilt was crushing every time I thought of Rick and my failure to protect Ava. I had spent five years trying to help her find the light after Jacob died. I watched her struggle and rage against me. In the end, I couldn't keep her safe and Rick died trying. The only person that could get through to Ava was Reid; I hadn't been enough. Not that I loved Ava the way Reid did. She was my dead best friend's wife, the woman I promised to take care of if he couldn't. I failed.

Reid's door swung open and his large frame came into view. "What are you doing out here?" he asked.

"Just about to knock on your door. You got a minute?"

"I have a few hours to kill. What's on your mind?"

He stepped back into his office and I followed him in, closing the door behind me. His office was another thing that had changed over the last year. Family pictures were now hung. Drawings and crafts that Melody and JJ had made were taped to the walls. Months ago he moved a table into the corner, so JJ could have a desk to do homework at when Reid had to pick him up from school for Ava. I couldn't lie and say it didn't gut me when Ava had started cutting me out of her and JJ's daily lives. Even before Reid had pulled his head out of his ass and claimed Ava, she was calling on him more and me less for help. Logically, I understood why Ava was trying to distance herself from me. I refused to allow her to pull into herself. I made her face her pain and grief and with every passing year she had hated me more and more for it.

I could take her anger. What I couldn't take was how broken and lost she was. She was a landmine and Reid was the one to finally disarm her.

"Don't go there, Mac," Reid said as he sat behind his desk.

"Go where?" I asked.

"The same fucking place you go every time you think about Rick. He died being the man we all knew him to be. Nothing that happened was your fault, or mine." I nodded in agreement even though I thought what he was saying was bullshit. I didn't have time for the argument. "On a side note, what the hell is up with the media dicks reporting the PC's daughter has been kidnapped before it's even hit radar?"

"Fuck if I know. Chief hadn't even reported it before I saw it on the news. Someone in his detail leaked it. There is no other way that the media would've caught the story."

"Unless Brown leaked it himself," Reid countered.

"Walk me through that. Why would Brown want the public to know his daughter was taken before his own department? A cop's family is in harm's way–all hands are on deck."

"Media doesn't ask the hard questions like; who would gain from the PC's daughter being kidnapped or, more to the point, who did the PC piss off enough to take his daughter? They just take a snippet and run with it–no facts necessary. Maybe the PC wanted it public because he needs the diversion and wanted the public on high alert. The city of San Francisco has now been tasked with finding Chief Brown's kidnapped daughter. Every wannabe sleuth out there is going to be looking. If nothing else but to get their name in the paper and a photo op with the PC."

"Goddamn it. Whoever leaked it just made my job a hundred times harder. There will be a thousand sightings of the girl all over the city. Resources are already fucked off because of the Holly Springs situation. The whole city is ready to pop off. You know Simmons? His cruiser was torched at the vigil. Some jackass threw a Molotov cocktail. I read the reports; shit went bad fast. From what I heard, Brown looked like he was gonna piss himself. Everyone talks. Everyone's heard the rumors, but no one will do shit about it because Brown's reach is far and wide. Well beyond SFPD."

"You want me to dig? Say the word; I'd be happy to reach out to some guys I know. Brown was investigated by internal affairs for misconduct twice before he took the job as *Top Cop*. He was dirty before he was PC and mark my words he's dirty now. Question is, how far are you willing to go? The boat isn't gonna rock, Mac. It's gonna fucking capsize."

I had been ignoring the rumors for a long time. Long enough that I was ashamed. I'd looked the other way on a lot, believing that, at the end of the day I was doing my job. I was making the streets safer. But was I really? Or was I now part of the problem?

"Capsize it," I told him.

"And blowback? I can't guarantee this won't get messy. Brown has eyes and ears everywhere."

"I cannot serve under a man that I know is dirty. I've turned the other way for too long. I'd rather hand in my shield."

Reid studied me before he added, "I'm talking about more than your shield."

"You're not the only one that is owed markers. I've gathered enough over the years that I'm not worried. Besides, that's why I keep the famous Logan Reid as a friend. No one is stupid enough to fuck with you."

"Jackass," Reid mumbled.

"Hate to change subjects but I need to talk to you about Laura," I started. Reid's face got hard, and his mouth turned down. It seemed she wasn't well liked at the moment. I couldn't blame him, but I was hoping to change that. "I've been seeing her for the better part of a year."

"Yeah? I gathered that much. Even though it wasn't you that told me. Right after that knowledge was imparted, I also found out she'd been cheatin' on you. I don't think there's much to talk about."

Damn. I hadn't thought that Reid would be pissed that I hadn't told him I was seeing Laura.

"Quinn Alexander is not her boyfriend. She lied. He's a Deputy US Marshal," I told him.

"What the fuck? Then why'd she say he was?"

"That's what I need to talk to you about."

For the next thirty minutes, I explained everything I knew about Harper Russo and her brother Frankie. Some of it was from Quinn, and the rest of the information was what I'd dug up on my own.

"Holy shit. That explains a lot," he replied, his expression clouded over. "I fucked up. Ever since I saw you and Laura together at the wedding, I'd been meaning to run her through the system. I knew there was something wrong. All of her answers were practiced; it felt like she had her past memorized instead of having memories. Something was off. Shit, man, I've been so wrapped up in my family, I let it slide. Sorry."

"There is nothing to be sorry for. I could've run her just as easily. I wanted her to tell me. I didn't want to dig for it. I've tried for months to get close to her, and she shuts me down around every turn. Every time I think I'm getting in, she reminds me it's just sex—nothing more. The day Quinn showed up at the café? I had made my decision to call her on all her shit and demand she tell me what was going on," I explained.

"Where do we go from here?" he asked.

There it was—Reid being the friend I knew him to be. He'd wade into the situation to help, no matter what the consequences.

"*We*, don't go anywhere. I need you clear of this. You have Ava and the kids to think about. I don't want to pull you in and put your family in danger. We're not talking about some petty lowlife here. Frankie Russo has a far reach and the money to get shit done. He put up a million dollars to have his kid sister whacked. His own flesh and blood. No way are you touching this. I just needed you to know what was going on."

Before I could tell him about what I found at Laura's house, he cut me off. "Fuck that noise. You know me better than that. Besides, I have resources you don't. My hands aren't tied with department procedures. You can't even put an APB out on her. What the fuck are you gonna do?"

"I've already had a meet with Nico Tuscani. I offered him a way to get to Russo."

"The fuck!" Reid thundered. "You had a meet with Tuscani alone? Jesus Christ, you know what it means to owe a fucking mobster a marker? He'll own you—for the rest of your life. Nico is ruthless—word is he's making moves to take back territory his father lost. That means there is about to be a war. A war he's gonna drag your ass into. Nico Tuscani does not skirt the law like Blaze and Iron Claw. He will not respect your boundaries like Blaze does. Nico will dirty you up so fucking fast and not give two shits when you go down."

Reid wasn't telling me anything I didn't already know. Everything he had told me, I had already thought of and made peace with.

"I can't let her die," I explained.

"I get that, brother. I don't want her to get hurt either. But, there has to be another way."

"No, you don't get it..." I was cut off when my phone started ringing. I quickly pulled it out, hoping it was Tuscani telling me he wanted to meet again.

Not recognizing the area code, I answered and was met with silence on the line.

"Hello?" I tried again.

I tuned the noises out around me and zeroed in on the breathing on the other end; it was faint and muffled. It was Laura, I knew it was. My heart rate kicked up and I strained to hear anything that would clue me in to where she was.

"I can hear you breathing. I can help you," I said,

lowering my voice. I tried to sound reassuring when I continued. "Just tell me where you are, and I'll come get you." The background noise was nearly silenced. She must've covered the mouthpiece with her hand. "Laura, please." I heard a muffled whimper and hurried to continue. "I know everything. I can help."

"How?" she whispered.

Perfect, she was talking. Now I had to convince her to let me help.

"Trust me, baby, I can make you safe," I promised.

"You can't. No one can. Just forget me, Mac."

Damn. She was getting ready to hang up. So damn independent.

"I'll never stop looking for you. I'll go to the ends of the earth to find you," I rushed out.

The line disconnected, and I turned to Reid. "She's at a truck stop. I could hear the traffic and the distinct sound of a Jake-brake."

Dustin entered Reid's office, laptop in hand. "Give me the number," he said before he had even sat down at a desk.

"She'll be gone before we trace it. There is no way she'd call from an unblocked number if she wasn't planning on leaving the location. Quinn taught her better than that."

I had to pray that was the case. I needed her to be smart until I could find her.

"It will give us a starting point," Reid said.

He wasn't getting it. There was no way he was coming with me.

I fingered Laura's necklace in my pocket. The small token made me feel a little closer to her.

6

SWEETEST TORTURE

Laura

He knew. Mac knew. Quinn must've panicked when I left and enlisted Mac's help to find me. In a moment of weakness, I had confided in him that I had feelings for Mac. I had to be smarter than this if I wanted to stay alive. Not that Quinn would knowingly put my life in danger; however, he had unwittingly altered the state of play.

Quinn didn't understand that Mac would put his life on the line to find me. I knew him, I'd watched him with Ava. Mac was fierce and hugely protective of those he loved. Not that he loved me; he didn't know me. But he was a man that would help anyone in danger. It was ingrained in him; he wore it like a second skin. I didn't want Mac to be involved—I wanted him to forget me. Find a nice normal woman and settle down. A woman that could give him a family. Selfishly, my heart constricted at the thought.

I slammed the handset back on the base and resisted the urge to bang it a few more times. There was no time to indulge in another pity party. I had to lock all my feelings down and concentrate on surviving. He'd forget me; he had to.

I went back into the truck stop's diner and looked around. As much as I needed to move, I also had to be careful. I glanced around, trying to find a woman truck driver. They were rare but did exist. When I didn't find a female, I went about looking for the safest looking man. My gaze landed on an older gentleman sitting at a table by himself. He was neatly dressed, reading the newspaper. I watched him for a few moments; I wasn't sure what I was looking for. It wasn't like he was going to stand up and announce to the restaurant he was a serial killer.

I had learned the hard way that looks could be deceiving. A murderer can wear five-thousand-dollar suits, and an innocent man can have a plethora of tattoos, whistle a creepy song, and eat pumpkin pie for breakfast. My brother was the prime example. He was educated, finely dressed, and he killed men, women, and children.

After careful consideration, I approached the man. "Excuse me, sir?"

The man looked up from his paper, and his eyes stayed on my face. No creepy perusal of my body. "Yes?" he asked.

"I'm sorry to bother you. I was wondering if you happened to be going north?" I asked.

He studied me for long moments before he answered. "Headed to Oregon," he answered.

"I was wondering if you'd mind a passenger. I can pay you for the ride," I told him and quickly added, "with cash." When his eyes narrowed.

"You in trouble with the law?" he asked. I shook my head. "There gonna be a man comin' around causing trouble?"

I thought about lying and telling him no, but there was something about this man that inspired honesty. He looked like someone's grandfather, and I didn't want to put him in harm's way.

"There could be. I'm sorry to have bothered you. Thank you for your time."

I'd have to find another way. I turned to leave when the man sighed and called out before I could get far. "Come sit down a minute." When I twisted to look at him, he gestured to the seat across from him. "Name's Steve."

I sat across from him, wrapping both hands around my to-go coffee cup. It had long run empty, but I needed something to hold onto. I was tired of this, running, lying, pretending not to care about anyone. I wanted it to end, but it never would. This was my life—my destiny.

"What's your name?" he asked.

I hadn't thought of what my new name was going to be and blurted out the first one that came to mind. "Aubrey," I answered.

"Nice to meet you, Aubrey. I didn't say no. I only want to know if I'm gonna have to shoot my way outta here." Steve smiled, obviously trying to make light of the situation.

"There's a strong possibility," I told him. He thought I was joking, but it was the God's honest truth.

"I'm not planning on leaving until tonight. I just pulled in and need to get some sleep. I'm pullin' out at nine tonight. Slot thirty-one. If you're interested, meet me at my rig. She's electric blue, *SE Trucking* on the side. You can't miss her," he offered.

That was nearly twelve hours from now. Twelve long hours, hours in which anything could happen. Other than my call to Mac, I'd been careful. I looked around the room again. I had no choice but to wait. As judgmental as it was, everyone else in the room creeped me out.

"I'd appreciate it," I thanked him before I stood and smiled. "I'll meet you there."

"Have you eaten?" he asked.

"I have, thank you," I lied.

He studied me once again; clearly he knew I wasn't telling the truth. My stomach was in knots, but I had to save every dime I could. Eating wasn't an option. "You run into any trouble before we pull out. You come find me."

That was nice of him to offer, but I wouldn't. My brother's soldiers didn't care who they hurt. Anyone who stood in their way died. Yet another reason I had to get as far away from Mac as I could.

I would never be able to live with myself if something happened to Mac because of me. Or Ava, Reid, and their kids. There was no room in my life for friendships.

"Thank you. I will."

On shaky legs, I walked back to the room I had rented last night. Once I was safely hidden, I let out a long exhale and flopped onto the hard bed. I needed to get some sleep if I was going to be awake all night driving. There was no way I could fall asleep in a truck with a man I didn't know. Even if he seemed nice.

I closed my eyes and thought of Mac.

When I opened the door to let Mac in, the first thing I noticed was his eyes. They were wild and troubled; a storm was brewing behind the deep blue orbs. Something had happened to make him call me and demand he come over. He rarely exerted his control outside of the bedroom. We had a contract firmly in place—limits and roles clearly defined.

He reached out and traced the gold links that circled my throat. A gift from him—a collar. He brushed my hair over my shoulder and goose bumps rose where he'd gently grazed my bare skin. With my hair out of the way, he had an unobstructed view of my breasts. My skin pebbled further when he traced a line from my collarbone down to my areola. My nipple hardened as he ran his finger around it before he gave me a hard pinch.

"You are beautiful. Do you hear me, Laura? Absolutely beautiful," he said. I hated that he called me Laura. I wanted to hear him call me by my real name. The name that my mother had given me.

My head snapped up, and my eyes once again searched his face for answers. Before I could analyze the emotion, it was gone. He schooled his features and continued his expert exploration of my body. I needed this time as much as Mac did. This was the only time I allowed myself to lose control. I could let go and know that Mac would take care of me. Not only physically but I could quiet my noisy mind and pretend I wasn't a fraud.

"Thank you," I whispered. "May I?" I glanced down at his already stiff cock.

"Yes, honey, you may," he answered.

I wasted no time working his zipper down and

pulled his cock out, not bothering to remove his pants or even push them down further than his thighs. I dropped to my knees in front of him and positioned him at my mouth. Without thought, I licked around his engorged head, losing myself in the taste of him. All too quickly he ended my fun and pulled his cock from my mouth. He bent, hoisted me up, and carried me to the kitchen table.

"Hands above your head," he demanded.

I did as he asked and my skin heated as he stared down at me, his gaze eating up every inch of my exposed skin. I spread my legs wider before he asked and shivered when his eyes flared in appreciation. A single swipe of his tongue over my pussy had me withering in anticipation. He stood and with a single thrust, he was fully seated inside of me. It didn't take him more than a few hard thrusts and I was panting. He knew he had me nearing orgasm and pulled out, letting his cock rest on my clit. I let out a groan of impatience and Mac smiled. His stare was smoldering as he took his cock in hand and teased around my entrance before he bent over and took my mouth in a bruising kiss, making sure his cock continued to rub my sensitive clit in sync with every brush of his tongue on mine.

I needed him closer and let my hands glide over his back even though he'd told me to put them over my head. "I need your cock, baby," I said against his lips.

"Greedy," he replied and reached between us, drag-

ging the head of his cock over my clit one last time before he pushed in again.

"Aiden," I groaned.

"Yes, honey?" he teased, only giving me the first couple inches of his cock.

"More. Harder. Please."

He stood back up, put both of my legs over his shoulders, and hit that perfect spot. He pounded into me, hard and rough. Just the way I liked it.

My orgasm built fast and furious. My hips bucked to meet his thrusts and I screamed my pleasure. A few more deep thrusts and he pulled out, jerking his cock. I watched as he marked me with his come. First on my belly, then on my breasts. The sight had my insides clenching. "Aiden," I moaned when the sexy show was over and let my head rest back on the kitchen table.

"Right here, honey," he answered.

Mac kissed over my scars, breaking the sex-fueled spell. I hated those scars. I hated that Mac always kissed them so reverently. Those scars reminded me of everything that was stolen from me. I knew he had questions about them. He had asked more than once now what they were from. I would never tell him. I would never tell anyone why I had them. They were disgusting and hideous. The day I got those scars my life had ended. Every dream, every hope, everything.

This was the hardest part of being with Mac. When

we were in a D/s scene or when we were having sex, it was easy. My mind was occupied. We were like two crazy people that couldn't get enough of each other's bodies.

I wasn't thinking about my past or my future. I wasn't trying my hardest to ignore his tender kisses. His soft touches. He deserved better than this. He needed more than I could ever give him. In a different life, he would've been the perfect man for me. I would've allowed myself to get lost in him. I wanted to get lost in him.

But I couldn't. It wasn't in my cards. I had been dealt a crap hand, and now all I could do was try my hardest not to lose what was left of my shitty life. I had to cut him loose and move on. I was a bad bet, that was for sure. And Mac was a good man and had already lost once. He didn't deserve what I was going to do to him.

"I'm sorry I was so short in my text message," Mac said against my skin. "It has been a shitty day. But, I shouldn't have demanded you be here."

"It's okay. I was more surprised is all. Ava and JJ okay?" I asked.

Mac and Ava had been bickering a lot lately. It didn't take a rocket scientist to figure out it was bothering Mac.

"Yeah. They are fine. Reid is actually with them now."

Well, if it didn't have to do with Ava, then I wasn't going to pry. It really wasn't my business. We shouldn't be talking at all. He came over, did incredible mind-boggling things to my body, then left. That was the way this was supposed to go. But more and more he stayed after to chat.

"Come here," Mac said and pulled me to a sitting position.

Before I knew what he was doing, he wrapped my legs around his waist and carried me to my bedroom. My common sense was screaming at me to make him leave, that this was the last thing on earth I needed to be doing, entertaining the idea of lying in bed curled into Mac. Allowing my mind to wish for things that I could never have.

"What's this?" Mac asked when he set me on my bed.

"What?" I returned, confused as to what he was referring to.

"This?" Mac held up my grandmother's scarlet emerald necklace.

So damn careless. I couldn't believe I had not put that away after I wore it the other night. That one necklace was all I had of my old life.

My grandparents owned a claim in the Wah Wah Mountains in Utah. When they were prospecting for uranium, back in the late fifties, they found scarlet emeralds instead. My grandfather had a necklace made for my grandmother as an anniversary gift. Five scarlet emeralds set in platinum. The large links that make up the chain have a patina that only comes after nearly sixty years.

"Oh, nothing. Just an old necklace," I answered.

"It looks like an antique."

I should've lied and told him it was a junky piece of costume jewelry. No personal information. That is what had kept me alive over the years. But, I couldn't bring myself to diminish my grandmother's memory that way. I loved her so much.

"It is. It was my grandmother's. It was her favorite. My grandfather had it made for her for their first wedding anniversary. It is all I have left of her," I explained, looking at the beautiful green gems sparkling as Mac dangled the necklace from his finger. "My most valued treasure," I admitted.

Mac had no idea the value of the necklace he was holding. Fair market price of scarlet emeralds were about ten thousand a carat. The necklace had five gems, all two carats in size. It was spectacular. If I closed my eyes, I could still picture my grandmother wearing it.

"You should be more careful with it then. Keep it locked up and not just laying on your nightstand." He gently set it back down.

He must have missed it earlier when he was over.

Oh, that's right, we never made it to the bedroom. We rarely did. The moment Mac walked into my house, we normally just ripped each other's clothes off in the living room.

"I took it out to look at it and forgot to put it away," I lied.

There was no way I was telling him that I had worn it to the ballet the other night. That was a special secret. Those nights were only for me. I could sneak away and get lost in the beauty of dance. I could sit in the audience and watch the performance. I could forget. But, once the curtain fell, all the pain and memories rushed back.

I sat up in bed, a sheen of sweat covering my shaking body. I came fully awake and reached for my throat, fingering the silver collar there. I both hated and loved dreaming of Mac; remembering our time together was the sweetest torture.

My grandmother's necklace.

I didn't have it. I forgot to get it from under my mattress. I'd been too busy crying about having to leave Mac I forgot the one thing I'd kept from my old life. I didn't care about the monetary value—its meaning was invaluable. Irreplaceable. I scrambled out of bed; I had to call Quinn. I hoped that the guys who had come to my house hadn't tossed the place. If they'd found it, it would be gone forever.

The last piece of my life would be... the knock on the door pulled me from my thoughts.

Shit. Had my brother's men found me? Panic flooded me; I had to think of a way to escape. There was nowhere to go. I broke another rule Quinn had taught me, always have a way out. This motel was the only place to lodge in the isolated area and they didn't have windows in the bathrooms. I was fucked. Completely and totally screwed. Without an escape route, I looked around for a weapon.

Nothing.

This was it. My past had finally caught up with me.

I was dead.

ITALIANS

Mac

"She's in Lake Tahoe, on the California side," Dustin said after he'd traced the number Laura had called from. "A truck stop called *Border Fuel*. It's literally on the border. A four hour and nineteen minute drive," he told me.

I stared at the map Dustin had up on his laptop. Four hours and nineteen minutes? I could be there closer to three if there wasn't traffic. I was formulating a plan when Reid interrupted my thoughts.

"Let's go. Dustin can manage things from here."

"I can't let you get involved. You have a family to think about," I reminded him.

"I do. And you're part of that family. You can stand here and argue with me or we can walk downstairs, get in your car, and drive to south Lake Tahoe and find your woman."

"Ava," I started.

"Will be devastated if something happens to you. And will be pissed as fuck she found out I let you go without backup. End of discussion, Mac. Get your ass in the car. We're wasting time."

Pushy bastard.

"Thanks, D," I said to Dustin and moved toward the door. Stopping, I turned to Reid. "Hey. Grab a secure burner phone."

Reid's eyes narrowed. "You think?" he asked.

"Not Alexander. Laura would've been dead long ago. But something's not right. I know it in my gut. Even with a million-dollar bounty, which is inspiration enough, it would've taken longer to find her. Someone else is in play. From what Quinn said, she's been successfully hiding on her own for years. And within hours of a hit being called in, she was found. She wouldn't have left without Quinn. They had a plan; she would've waited. He was setting up a safe house. She left in such a hurry she left something special behind, a necklace."

Without questioning me, Reid reached in his desk and grabbed two phones and followed me down to my car. After fishing Quinn's card out of my pocket, Reid handed me a phone and I dialed the man's number, knowing I needed to apologize for being a dick.

"Deputy Alexander," he answered.

"It's Mac," I greeted.

"You get one, too?" he inquired, not using Laura's name or asking outright about the phone call.

"I did. I need to apologize. I was a dick and you were right; my head was up my own ass." I was actually more embarrassed that I had been so blinded by jealousy I'd lost my temper and made myself look like an ass and possibly put Laura in more danger. I wonder if I hadn't stormed off and demanded that Laura talk to me if she would've caved and told me the truth about who she was and the threat she'd lived with.

"No need," he easily accepted. "Missed my call. I'm wrapped up in something that's unavoidable," he told me.

"I didn't miss mine. Maybe you should call me back when you get somewhere private. I'm good on my end," I told him.

"Are you driving?" Quinn inquired.

"About to. I have a few days off—thought I'd get some fresh air." I looked at Reid; he was looking around the parking lot, his hand going to the gun at his side. Reid nodded toward the street, gesturing to a car. "Seems I have company. I'd better go. Call when you can."

I abruptly disconnected, reaching for my weapon as well. There was a black sedan parked. Two men sat inside, dark complexion, dark hair, watching us.

Italians.

"You think they followed me here, or is my car tracked?" I asked.

"Hard to say. You think those are Russo's men or Tuscani's?"

Good fucking question. I dialed Tuscani. When his angry voice answered, I ignored his greeting.

"This is Mac. You got men on me?" I cut straight to it.

"You've got some balls, detective, calling my personal number asking me some shit," he returned.

"Balls or not, Tuscani, you better answer my fucking question. I'm looking at two Italian men watching me. You gotta know, I'm making my move in two minutes. If they're yours and you want them back, I suggest you speak up."

"I see. Because they're Italian, they have to be mine." He chuckled.

"You're down to one minute. They fucking yours?" I asked again.

"No. But a friendly warning, you're on radar. There's money on your head, too."

"How do you know?"

"I did some digging after you left. You're both fucked."

If I didn't need Nico's help, I would've crawled so far up his ass and jammed him up on any charges I could make stick. However, I held my temper in check, knowing that he was my only hope of saving Laura.

"What'd you find?" I ground out.

Nico chuckled before he said, "Russo himself saw Harper on the news. He outsourced that shit fast; he wants her dead. Big mistake going to her house; you should've left it alone. They think you're the man that's been hiding her. Watch your back."

I didn't bother replying and disconnected, turning my attention back to Reid.

"Dustin is ready to lay down cover while we get to my car. On three," he told me.

Reid counted us down and we ran across the lot to his Rover. Gunfire rang out as Reid gunned it out of the lot. The cell in my hand rang and Reid put it through the speakers.

"No casualties. Both men fled on foot. How do you want to handle this?" Dustin asked.

"Watch the car. Don't approach. See if you can run the plate and CCTV in the area. I want to know how they followed Mac. Also, pull Mac's truck into the garage and see if there is a tracker. Keep everything you find. No use destroying the tracker if you find one. They already know where his truck is. Also, call Austin. I want him sitting on my house. Shoot any fucker that approaches—I mean, anyone. I'll call Blaze."

Reid pushed the end button on his steering wheel and I watched as his jaw ticked.

"This is why I want you clear of this," I bit out. "I'll drop you at home, where you should be."

"I'm not clear of this. Two mother fuckers were sitting outside my office. If they know you, they know me. There is not a goddamn person in San Francisco that doesn't know we're connected."

"Mother fucker." I fought the urge to slam my fist into the dash.

Three hours and thirty minutes later, we were pulling into the parking lot of *Border Fuel*. It looked like any other truck stop across the U.S. It wasn't as dirty as some, nor was it a five-star hotel.

My gut clenched at the thought of Laura staying in some unsafe no-tell-motel with trained killers after her. We exited Reid's Rover and all the fine hairs on the back of my neck stood on end. A tingling of awareness coursed through my veins.

"She's close," I announced.

A hundred dollars later, the guy at the desk had given me Laura's room number—dick. He better hope to God he was telling the truth and no one else had been by looking for her. If something had happened to her in that room, I'd strangle his ass.

I found the room and knocked. Reid stood to the side, scanning the parking lot for any unwanted attention, or visitors.

Then I heard it, a loud bang on the wall and a scream. Reid's attention snapped to me as I took my leather coat off and wrapped it around my arm, slamming my fist through the motel window. Using my jacket, I cleared away the jagged pieces, yanking the curtains down at the same time. Laura was standing across the small room, holding her face. A man was next to her, poised to strike again. I was through the window and tackling the man before he could hit her any more.

My vision blurred, and red-hot rage took over. I felt the first punch connect with the man's face and faintly heard bone crushing under the roaring in my ears. I didn't feel the second or the third; hell, there may have been a hundred. Nothing registered until Reid was hauling me back, yelling in my face.

"Enough."

I looked around at the carnage; a man lay unconscious on the floor, my hands covered in his blood. Laura's back was to the wall; she was shaking and covering her mouth with both hands.

"You okay?" I asked, noting her shirt was slightly

ripped. The red mark on her face was clearly the mother fucker's handprint.

"You shouldn't be here," she whispered.

Her words pissed me off. "Why's that? If we hadn't shown up, you would likely be the one half dead on the floor," I returned.

"You can't be here. They'll find you. You have to let me go," she begged.

She still didn't trust me after all this time. I felt those words deep in my gut. There was a split second I thought about calling Alexander, telling him where he could find her, and leaving it to him. Her next statement stopped me.

"I couldn't live with myself if my brother hurt you." On a slow blink, she continued, "I'd rather die than live knowing I put you in danger."

"Babe, come here." She didn't, so I repeated, "Harper. Come. Here."

Her head snapped up at the use of her real name and a look I had never seen before replaced the shock of hearing it. I felt that, too, only that look hit me in the chest. Without further prompting, she stepped around the man on the floor and burrowed close.

"I promise I'll keep you safe."

8

———

I'D RATHER DIE

Laura

I heard his words but didn't believe them. Not because I didn't think he meant them; I knew he did. However, I knew my brother. I knew the lengths he'd go to kill me. I was a rat, and in his world the only option was death. He had to kill me. If he didn't, he'd look weak, and if he looked weak, *he* was as good as dead.

One of us had to die–it was the only way.

Reid's phone rang, and he pulled it out of his pocket, checking the caller ID before sliding his finger across the screen to answer. "Go," he greeted. "Right. ETA? Fuck. Yeah, we got her."

"Time to go. We got company–five minutes out."

"You both should go," I tried again.

I'd rather die alone in the ratty motel room than have either of them hurt.

"Straight up, we do not have time to debate this. Move your ass, grab your shit, and get to the car," Reid barked.

"Think of Ava and your family," I said to Reid, trying to appeal to his rational side. He loved Ava and his kids. He'd never put them in harm's way, ever.

"Right. I see you're not getting this. I hate to do this now but again, you're not getting it so here it is. We got less than five minutes to be gone before some seriously fucked up mobsters get here. There's a million-dollar price on your head, and Mac's got money on his, too. I'm thinking the men who are on their way want that payout. We're here, we're in it, and we're not leaving you behind. So, your choices are: stand here and fucking talk about it and risk bloodshed or move your ass to the car so Mac can keep his shield. Choice is yours. Either way, we're not leaving you," Reid explained.

"What?" I screeched. Yes, I screeched, sounding like a prepubescent boy even to my own ears. "He put a hit out on you?" That last part was even more shrill.

"Fuck it," Mac said. He bent, put his shoulder to my stomach, stood, and lifted me into a fireman's hold and said to Reid, "Grab her shit."

I was moving to the car. Not on my own two feet

but Mac was carrying me. That pissed me off. Partly because he was acting like a caveman, but mostly because I wanted them to listen to me and leave. They didn't understand what my brother was capable of. I did.

Mac opened the car door, my ass hit the seat, and the door slammed closed just as the front two opened. My bag was tossed into the back seat with me and Reid started the car.

That was it. No more discussion. Mac had gotten his way. I closed my eyes at the thought that they were both signing their own death warrants. Being anywhere near me was dangerous. My brother was brutal; there was no one worse. After my brother took over the family, I was able to turn a blind eye, mostly. But the day I came home on an unexpected visit and saw what he was doing, I could no longer. Once I saw with my own eyes the monster he'd become, I had a choice. And my choice was to deflect. Completely and totally. My brother, being the dick he was, didn't like my choice. He really didn't like that I'd lived after he thought he'd left me for dead.

Now there was a price on Mac's head. Fucking, fucking, Frankie.

A phone rang, and Mac grabbed it from the cup holder between him and Reid. He didn't look at the screen long before he slid his finger across the smooth glass and put it on speaker.

"Mac," he answered.

"You got the package?" Quinn's voice boomed through the speaker.

I fought back the urge to yell at Quinn for getting Mac involved.

"Yes," Mac clipped.

"Good. I'm going to be out of reach for a while—work-related. I trust you have the situation under control?"

"I do," Mac answered.

"I'll be in touch when I can. Tell her I hope she understands why I told you."

Before Mac could answer, Quinn disconnected.

"Lie flat across the back seat," Mac instructed, twisting in his seat to look at me. He winced and added. "We'll stop and get some ice for your face as soon as we can."

My hand came up to my face. I had forgotten that son-of-a-bitch had hit me. How had I been so wrong?

"Who was in your room?" Reid asked.

"His name was Steve," I told him once I got myself situated in the back seat.

I didn't want to talk about him, how wrong I'd been to trust him and his kind eyes. I hated to admit it but another piece of me broke. What was wrong with the human race? I'd attempted to keep my faith in humanity even after my own family tried to kill me. I tried my hardest to believe that everyone wasn't lying and weren't out to hurt you.

"What was he doing in your room?" Mac questioned.

I closed my eyes and shook my head. Mac was going to be pissed—really pissed. I tried to change the subject. "I need to find a passport. I think I should go north into Canada."

"Christ. That's not happening. Why was Steve in your room?" Mac bit out.

No way was I telling him that. He'd lose his ever-loving mind.

"Seriously, Mac. I was only staying in that shit hole because I had to toss my last identity. I will be safe in Canada. Frankie doesn't have reach out of the country," I lied. "And you'll be safe once you're away from me." I prayed that last part was true. Maybe my brother's hitmen would lose interest in Mac once they figured out that he couldn't lead them to me.

"Serious as shit! Why the fuck was that man in your goddamned room?" Mac all but shouted.

Mac's temper didn't seem to have the same impact on Reid that it had on me. Reid never flinched and remained silent as he continued to drive us down the highway, unaffected by Mac's outburst.

"He was going to drive me to Oregon," I rushed out.

"Come again?" Mac growled, and I fought back a shiver. I loved when his voice got deep and rumbly.

"He was going to drive me to Oregon?" I repeated, this time posing it as a question.

When Mac didn't speak for several minutes I spoke, mainly to break the silence. "Aiden?" I wasn't sure how I was going to justify my folly, but I had to try.

"Don't. I am fighting back the urge to commit murder at the same time trying not to pull you over my knee in a moving vehicle and redden your ass for being so foolish. He could've raped you."

His words made me flinch. That was exactly what Steve was trying to do. Not that I would confirm that to Mac in his present state of mind. However, I didn't need him reminding me of the fact when I had lived it not thirty minutes ago. To think I'd felt relief when I heard Steve's voice outside the hotel room door and not my brother's men. I let him in. I'd happily opened my door to a man that wanted to violate me. I was so stupid. If Mac and Reid hadn't shown up when they did... I couldn't let my mind go there. I had to stay focused on my current situation and not the *what-ifs*.

"Good thing you're done with that shit. No more hitchhiking with fucking truckers."

"You're right. I'll be more careful."

The growl that came from Mac was not the kind that made my belly whoosh; he sounded like a frustrated wild beast getting ready to kill its prey. "Jesus, Laura. Pull your head out of your ass. There won't be a next time for you to be more careful. When I said you're done with that shit, I meant—*you are done*. No more running. No more hiding. And definitely no more going at it alone."

If it was possible for my heart to actually break a rib from pounding so hard, there was no doubt I'd have a few cracked. Mac had no idea what he was saying. I couldn't stop running. My brother would never stop, and he'd kill anyone who got in his way. I'd seen it firsthand. I'd hid in the shadows of my family home and watched my brother kill a young boy right before he tortured the boy's mother. The woman's husband, the boy's father, sat tied to a chair, bloodied and beaten, begging for Frankie to stop. Even Frankie's men grimaced as he delivered blow after blow to the woman. The same way he beat me. He was relentless.

"Breathe, baby," Mac cooed, reaching in the back seat, grabbing my hand. "I won't let anyone hurt you."

"You can't stop them," I explained.

I watched as Mac's face got hard, his normally kissable lips flattening into two thin lines. "You don't trust I can keep you safe?"

I shook my head. He wasn't getting it. It didn't matter how much I trusted Mac, Frankie would find a way to kill us all. He wouldn't care that Mac was a cop, or Reid was some badass private investigator, or Ava and Reid's kids were sweet and innocent.

Frankie Russo would rain hellfire down and kill every last one of us. I had to find a way to escape.

I fell silent for the long drive back to the city. Most of the drive, I pretended I was asleep and there wasn't much verbal communication between Reid and Mac either. The few times I cracked my eyes open, Mac was on his phone, tapping on the screen. I took the opportunity to study his profile, memorizing the fine lines around his eyes, how his brow crinkled when he was concentrating, how his nose had a perfect slope leading to a pair of lips that I knew from experience could do the most mind-blowing things.

All the while I laid in the back seat and plotted my escape. Now I was not only running from my deranged brother but the man that was quite possibly the love of my life.

I hated Frankie fucking Russo.

9

IT'S WAY OVER

Mac

Reid was being unusually quiet on the drive, allowing me time in my head to sort my shit out. Laura had all but admitted she didn't trust me. She didn't believe I could keep her alive. As much as it pissed me the fuck off, I couldn't blame her. She had been around when I let Ava and JJ down. Ava had been kidnapped on my watch, by Carl—a fellow cop. I'd missed all the signs. I hadn't noticed that Ava was being stalked and a crazy man was planning on taking her so he could live out some sick and twisted fantasy. Yeah, Laura knew all about Carl, and how Rick had also died because of my shortcomings. If I hadn't been so wrapped up in my own shit, I would've noticed the sick fuck had stolen Ava's spare key I'd kept in my desk at the station. He'd made a copy and used it to let himself into her house.

My stomach rolled at the memory, at the thought of what he'd been doing alone in her house. That was on me, and it would never matter Ava said she didn't blame me, that it wasn't my fault—it was. I was careless and Ava, JJ, Reid, and ultimately, Rick had paid the price.

I was about to ask Reid if he'd put Austin and Dustin on Laura until I could get the situation with Russo under control when he rolled to a stop in front of a house.

"Where are we?" I asked when Reid pulled the keys out of the ignition.

"A safe house," he replied. I took in my surroundings and cocked my head. "There are places even you don't know I own," Reid explained.

"Austin and Dustin available?" I asked.

"Nope."

Before I could question Reid as to why his men were unavailable, he was out of his truck and opening the door for Laura.

What the fuck?

Reid led us into the house, disarmed the alarm, rattled off the code, and cruised into the kitchen, leaving Laura and me in the foyer.

For the first time since I had met Laura, I didn't know what to say to her. I was dumbstruck and the hell of it was all I wanted to do was comfort her and tell her that she would be okay. Promise her that I wouldn't let Russo or his men near her. But I couldn't. Her bottom lip started to quiver; the tiny movement revealing just how scared she was. That pissed me off. Laura was strong, to a fault, never allowing her true emotions to the surface. Two strides and I was in her space. Her head tilted back to look at me, her face softening, and I was beating back the urge to take her mouth. Her amber eyes glistened with unshed tears and my hands moved to cup her cheeks.

"Everything will be fine," I whispered.

"I don't want you to get hurt."

She kept saying that. Her concern for my safety was appreciated but it was starting to irritate me.

"You don't think I can take care of you? Of myself?"

"You don't understand what he's like. What he's capable of."

"Right. So you don't trust me."

"It's not that..." she trailed off.

Reid came back into the room, derailing our conversation.

"I'll send Roni out to pick you up some food. I'll also have her drop off some clothes and a secure laptop for you," Reid said, coming to a stop in front of us. "And another burner phone for Laura."

For a split second, I questioned Reid's logic,

sending his untrained secretary out for provisions. But she was perfect actually. If someone was watching, no one would pay attention to the unassuming woman.

"A word before I leave?" Reid asked and jerked his head toward the door. "See you soon, Laura." He offered her a smile.

She gave him a small wobbly smile in return and stepped around us, making her way to the worn blue corduroy recliner. She sat, pulling her feet up and tucked them into the armrest, her bent legs pulled up tight against her chest; she rested her chin on her knee and commenced staring at the wall. Now more than ever I wished I knew what was going on in her pretty little head.

I followed Reid outside and closed the door, praying Laura wasn't planning her escape out the back door. I didn't like that I couldn't see her, but the privacy was necessary.

"I'm gonna lay it out for you, brother. The same way you did when I was battling it out with Ava. Pull your head outta your ass and fix this." Reid's hand shot up, stopping me from speaking over him. "Enough already. It was enough six years ago when Jacob died. It was over last year when Ava and I got together. And it's *way* over now. You are going to let misplaced guilt eat at you until you throw away a good woman who needs you."

It was a low-blow bringing up Jacob, Ava's first husband and my best friend. Reid was wrong—I wasn't holding onto misplaced guilt. It was firmly where it was supposed to be—on my shoulders. Jacob died alone in an alley, killed by his own brother after finding out his blood was a gangbanger and was stealing and selling heroin. Jacob was my partner. I should've been there. And in the years after his death, I had, in fact, failed at keeping Ava and Jacob afloat. I was too deep in my own grief to sort Ava out and I allowed her to push me away. It wasn't until Reid came along that Ava truly began to heal.

"You heard her. She doesn't trust me."

"No. That's what *you* heard. That is not what I heard. What I heard was a woman who is deathly afraid of her brother. I heard a woman who is petrified the man she loves will put himself in danger if he sticks close. You're hearing shit you want to hear so you can continue to beat yourself up. Give it up, Mac. You did right by Ava and JJ. You did right by Jacob. It's fucking painful watching you beat yourself up. And, man, if you don't think Ava sees it, too, you are wrong. It kills her that because she couldn't pull her shit together you blame yourself. You ever stop to think that it wasn't supposed to be you that brought the shine back to my woman's eyes? That maybe that was for me? That *I* was meant to be the one to give her what she needed to move on. In all this time you've been locked away in your head, you ever stop to fucking think that was *our* journey? Mine and Ava's. So again, pull your fucking head out of your ass and fix your shit. She needs you. She needs your head straight and you on the top of your game. She's right about one thing—Frankie Russo is not to be underestimated. He's a sick fucker and now both of you are in the line of fire. And, Mac, I'll be goddamned if I let you get dead. You know I have your back, in every way. That includes helping you pull... your... head... out...of....your ass."

Fuck! Fuck! Fuck.

"I'll leave you with that, brother. Chew on it. I'll be back around later to check on you two. Expect Roni in a few hours. Until then, I suggest you work out some of that pent-up frustration. It might help with your sunny disposition." Reid chuckled and hoofed it down the driveway back to his Rover. I watched him get in and drive away, then I stared into the empty street wondering what the fuck had just happened. On an exhale, I opened the front door and was pleased to see Laura right where I'd left her.

"I need to make a call." Her eyes came to me but other than that Laura didn't move. "After that, we need to talk." She nodded and closed her eyes, hiding herself from me.

I moved to the kitchen and returned the text that

Nico had sent earlier. He was more than happy to take care of Frankie Russo and that included the two men that were in San Francisco to take out Laura. It was in his best interest and would end up being quite profitable for him. Russo's Long Island territory had been thriving since the death of Laura's father and Russo's restructuring. Nico assured me that the job would be done in less than twenty-four hours and the hit would be called off sooner. I didn't ask for details and he didn't offer them. At the end of the day, I was still a cop, and I had already jumped so far over the line I could no longer see any remnants of it. I was already making deals with a mob boss; the less I knew about the actual plan the better. Once the threat was eliminated, I would meet with Nico to discuss his payment. I was fucked, and I knew it. Frankie Russo might've been a twisted ruthless son-of-a-bitch, but Nico Tuscani was only a half-step down and no less ruthless.

It was times like these I really wished I hadn't quit smoking. I would give my left arm to feel the calm after a long drag of nicotine. Sometimes after a shift or a really shitty case, Jacob would join me for a cigarette before he went home to Ava and JJ. We'd catch a smoke on the back steps of the precinct and we'd decompress. Jacob always looked at the bright side of life. The silver lining, he called it. He could take any fucked-up situation and make you see one good thing in it. I needed that now. I needed his help in the worst way. Damn, I missed him. Good cop, good husband, and great fucking dad. He loved his boy. But loved Ava more. He loved Ava in a way that was rooted down into his bones. Jacob understood that he had to love Ava that much to ensure that his son got everything he needed from his mother. He filled her with so much love and in turn, she filled the house with it. When he died, she shattered. As the years passed, her anger and resentment toward me grew until she was openly hostile. I knew she needed someone to blame, someone to lash out, but it fucking burned my gut. Now she had Reid and she was happy. She had her bright playful smile back. Reid loved her much the same way Jacob had. They both understood what they had in a good woman and went to great lengths to protect her. In turn, she gave them the greatest gift a man could ask for —a beautiful life.

Had I been a self-absorbed narcissistic prick? Thinking that Ava's pain was all about me and mine to fix? I would've never been able to give Ava what she needed to move on. I loved her like a sister, not a woman. There were times she cried in my arms but the way I cared for her was vastly different from a man who was caring for a woman he deeply loved. Maybe Reid was right about one thing; I wasn't meant to be the one to bring her back to life. She was Reid's. And she came alive under his care. But I was meant to be the one to protect her. I had given my word to Jacob.

I knew Reid was correct about one more thing; if I didn't stop behaving like a pansy-assed fool I was going to lose Laura, and if I wasn't on my game, it might be in a permanent way. I couldn't let Laura down. However, I couldn't reconcile how she would ever trust me to be the man to protect her.

All the fine hairs on the back of my neck tingled and I turned.

"Mac?" Laura whispered from the doorway.

"Yeah, baby?"

"I need you," she said, still whispering.

My heart rate kicked up and my muscles tightened. I hoped like hell I wasn't misreading what Laura was saying.

"What do you need?"

"You. Just you."

I didn't ask for further clarification. Her breathy words and needy eyes told me everything I needed to know. I had read the situation right. Now the only question was, how much of myself did I give?

10

HARPER

Laura

Before I could blink, Mac was on me, his finger tracing the silver around my neck.

"You kept it." I didn't think that was a question, more an observation, so I didn't answer. Instead, I soaked in his strength as he wrapped his hand around the back of my neck and squeezed, his thumb now grazing the soft skin at the side of my neck.

"Aiden."

"Before we go upstairs, I need to make sure you understand what you're asking."

Oh, no. I didn't want to understand. I didn't want to think. That was the whole point of me kneeling at his feet. He thought he was in control. All I had to do was let go and be.

"No more secrets. No more hiding. You are mine.

Mine to protect, mine to own, and mine to love. I will not let you hide from me anymore. If I'm giving you all of me, I'm damn well taking all of you. And, Laura, by taking I mean, you giving yourself freely to me. Are you ready for that?"

The words stuck in my throat. Could I give him all of me? I wanted to. I wanted nothing more than to belong to Aiden Mackenzie. But I couldn't. Frankie would kill him. Or he'd kill me, leaving Mac with nothing but guilt and pain. He already shouldered more than he should. He carried guilt over what had happened to Ava. He never said it, but I could see it. I could feel it rolling off of him in waves, especially right after Reid got Ava back after she was kidnapped. I had been on the receiving end of his dominance as he tried to regain control. It was magnificent and perfect. However, it broke my heart to see him so detached and methodical. I thought at the time he had finally understood I didn't want the emotional connection he had offered. I only wanted what he could wring from my body. But once I had that side of him, I wanted my old Mac back. Especially when I caught on to why he had pulled away. I had missed his soft touches, the way he took care of me, cuddled me close, whispering sweet words. How he had always tucked me into bed if he was leaving at night. I, of course, fought those advances at the time, not wanting to admit to myself I cherished them. Needed them. Would miss them when I inevitably had to run.

I shook my head, not trusting my voice and watched as Mac's face turned to stone. His normal gentle blue eyes turned stormy. Anger and something else swirling together.

"I see," he said and pulled his hand away from my neck, stepping back.

"No, you don't see. That's the problem. You've never seen."

"What haven't I seen, Laura?" he demanded.

I hated that name. I hated every fucking thing it meant.

"That's not my name!" I yelled.

And then the dam broke.

Everything I didn't want Mac to know came spewing out in a tidal wave of indignation and resentment. "I hate that name. Number seventeen. At first, I picked my new names with care. Something pretty. Somewhere around name ten, I stopped caring. It didn't matter how pretty my new name was, my life was still ugly. Frankie had made sure of it. He made sure he took everything I loved. Did you know I went back to Long Island to pick up my pointe shoes? Fucking shoes. I had ten other pairs at home in the city, but I wanted that pair. They were my favorite. I went home and watched my brother shoot a child, then turn his monstrous hands on a woman and beat her. He killed a little brown-haired boy because his father hadn't paid a debt. Wanna know how much? Five thousand measly fucking dollars. Five, Mac! Five, five, five..." I screamed.

"Baby," Mac whispered and reached for me.

"No." I pulled away. "You want my secrets—fine. You can have them all. I don't want them anymore. I don't want this life! This isn't my life. I had a life and it was perfect. I should've known it would be taken away. I didn't deserve it. I have Russo blood in my veins—evil, nasty, tainted blood. Frankie made a grave mistake the night he thought he was going to teach me about family loyalty. He started by taking away the one thing that mattered to me most in the world. Once he broke my legs, I had nothing more to lose. Nothing to live for. There's my secret, Mac. I'm a mafia princess. Still want me? My brother is serving a life sentence in a federal penitentiary because I'm a rat. How 'bout now? And if that wasn't enough, there is a million-dollar price tag on my head. I'm a bad bet, Mac. Cut your losses and walk away."

"A ballerina," Mac said, and my heart squeezed. "Long toned perfect legs."

Anger welled in my belly and bubbled up into my throat, threatening to choke me. "Perfect?" I spat, the word tasting like bile on my tongue. "Frankie made sure they'd never be *perfect* again."

"I can see it. You in a beautiful dress with layers of silk and soft lace. Graceful and fluid in your movements. Stunningly beautiful on stage, holding the audience captive with your elegance."

"Stop."

"Trust me to take care of you."

I shook my head.

"Trust me," he semi-repeated.

He was being a hard-headed man. He couldn't fix this for me. There was no changing my life. I realized it didn't matter what I told him, how I tried to explain it, he was never going to listen to me.

"Harper!" he growled.

My eyes shot to his as they narrowed on me. His jaw was ticking, and I could see his heartbeat pounding on the side of his neck.

"He'll kill you. He'll find you and kill you."

"I won't let that happen." Damn stubborn ass man.

"You think that. But unless you've been hiding a cape somewhere, his men will find you. They'll use you to get to me. How can you want me to live with that? If something happens to you, I will let them kill me. I won't live knowing you died because of me. I can't, Aiden. I can't. I hate my brother. I detest the monster he is. I loathe the mob. But the thing I despise him most for—is taking you from me."

Mac didn't let me finish. His lips were on mine, demanding entrance. This wasn't a soft and enticing kiss. This was something more; demanding, rough, possessing. He swung me into his arms like he had hundreds of times and stalked up the stairs, breaking the kiss to lie me on the bed.

"Trust me," he demanded. He pulled his shirt over his head and casually tossed it aside. "I'll keep you safe." He toed off his boots and off came his jeans, pulling his boxers down with them. "I promise no one will hurt you again. I can't lose you, baby. I lived it for two days and I was going out of my goddamned mind. Trust me to keep us both safe and stay here with me. Stay and let me love you." There Mac stood, completely unmasked, staring down at me. Vulnerable. He wasn't hiding anything from me. Not his body, not his thoughts, not even his love for me.

"I'm scared."

Mac pulled off my shoes and let them fall on the floor. His hands went to the button of my pants and made quick work of unbuttoning them, pulling the zipper, and dragging them down my legs, divesting me of my panties with them.

"So beautiful," he murmured.

So horrid was more like it.

"Exquisite," he said, lifting my leg and kissing my ankle, stopping at the beginning of my long surgical scar. I tried to pull my leg away and his grip tightened. "My beautiful Harper, the ballerina."

"Stop," I begged as he kissed over my scar.

"Talented. Determined. So fucking strong." Mac kissed up my thigh, my pelvis, over my belly button, pushing my shirt up as he went. He stopped, gathering it above my breasts. "Trust. Me."

The cool air of the room made my nipples pucker as he pulled the cups of my bra down, pushing my breasts together and putting them on display. His tongue lashed out, leaving a wet trail over my nipple that had my back bowing, reaching for more.

My skin heated as his thick cock hardened on my thigh. Yes. This was what I needed. No more talking. I spread my legs, trying to maneuver him where I wanted. Mac's teeth clamped down on my nipple, halting my movements.

"Do. Not. Move." The command in his voice caused an involuntary tremor to rock through my body. Mac lowered his head and went back to lavishing my breasts with careful attention. When he was done thoroughly working me up to a fevered pitch, he moved over me, settling into the cradle of my hips. Yet, he still didn't take me. Both hands came to my face, forcing me to look at him. There was no escaping his penetrating stare. No hiding.

This was Mac. Always demanding my full attention.

"I want you to listen carefully, Harper. I've decided I'm no longer asking. I'm taking. This..." he stopped and fingered my collar, "means that you already trust me. You've already handed your safety and care over to me. And deep down inside, even if you can't admit it out loud, you know it's true. You trust me with your body, the gift of your submission, and you sure as shit know down to your bones I will protect you with my life. You recognize it, and that's why you're scared. But I promise you, baby, I will protect you. And if I die trying? That is my choice to make. You're not pushing me away. You're not running. You are not alone. Not anymore."

Mac gently brushed the tear off my cheek and then swept his lips against mine. It was a soft touch, tender, and so damn sweet more tears fell.

I wasn't sure if it was relief or fear and Mac didn't give me a chance to explore those feelings too long before he slid inside me. Giving me slow long strokes, he held my gaze, not allowing me to break eye contact.

Possession.

Total and complete possession. Everything he had said was the truth. I knew that he would protect me at the expense of his own life and that scared me the most.

My hips moved and synced with the now demanding pace of Mac's thrusts. The growl that answered my purr sent shockwaves through my body. The erotic symphony of grunts and moans filled the room, intensifying my desire.

"So slick," Mac groaned, sliding one hand under my ass. "Hands, Harper. I want you to touch me."

On his command, my hands snaked around his back. My nails scored his skin as I explored his hard muscles, flexing and contracting with exertion under my fingertips. His thrusts quickened and the slow burn he was building turned fast and incendiary. The throbbing started and a fine sheen of sweat coated my skin.

"Aiden," I panted.

"I'm with you, baby. Hold on a little longer."

Mac adjusted his angle and I couldn't hold out. The explosion detonated, and my vision blurred.

"Please," I forced out.

"Fuck. Harper!" Mac slammed into me and stayed planted deep. "So good, baby."

His cock swelled and throbbed as he joined me in ecstasy. Our orgasms mingled together, coating his dick as he slowly glided in and out.

Coming to a stop, and with a lingering kiss, he announced, "Be back."

I lost his cock but got his lips again, in a soft brush across my throat above my collar. A touch that was familiar and comforting. My legs didn't loosen even though Mac was trying to disengage. I didn't want him to move. I didn't want to lose the connection and safety I had when he was close.

When his gaze came up from my neck to meet mine, he gave me a lazy smile. It was cocky and full of mirth. "I love that you wanna keep those sexy legs wrapped around me. But, baby, I'm hungry and need to clean you up before I eat."

He winked and broke the lock my legs had around his waist. He disappeared into the bathroom, coming back to the bed with a washcloth in his hand. Mac was thorough; gently washing my most private parts. Through it all, I kept my legs spread wide for him. His hungry regard only gave him more to clean as a fresh wave of lust rushed through my body.

"Fuck," Mac muttered and traced my opening with a long, thick finger; dipping it in my pussy just a fraction before pulling it out, spreading moisture up to my clit. "So fucking sexy." Mac finished with the washcloth and carelessly tossed it aside before he climbed back onto the bed, stretching out next to me, propping his head on a bent elbow, his other hand gently trailing up and down my hip. "There is never an hour, a minute, a second of the day, I don't dream about when

I can sink back into you and fuck you into oblivion. You make me forget the world, Harper. When I'm surrounded in your heat, nothing else exists. Nothing matters but what we create. I'm never letting you go. If I have to quit my job and run with you, I will. There is nothing in my life that matters the way you do."

I could feel his eyes on me, but I didn't dare meet his stare. The terror and excitement mixed together in a content beat of juxtaposition. Despite or maybe because of how much I loved Mac, I struggled with staying. It was selfish to keep him, even though I wanted nothing more than to wrap myself in the safety he offered. I was scared to death.

"You don't even know me."

Everything had been a lie.

11

HOLD ON

Mac

"I know you."

"You didn't even know my name," she murmured as if that meant a goddamned thing. Now she was just being difficult to be difficult.

"I don't need to know your name to know your heart. Laura, Harper, fucking Mary Jo Anderson, your name doesn't mean jack shit to me. Your past doesn't mean jack shit. Your brother, the family you were born into, none of that matters now. I know *you* and that's what matters."

Laura slowly raised her eyes to meet mine.

Harper.

I had to start thinking of her as Harper.

"What's your name now?" The thought struck me that before I started down the path of calling her

Harper, I should find out what alias her and Quinn had decided on.

"Huh?"

"Your new name. You ditched Laura. I'm assuming you and Quinn picked a new one."

"Ohh." She scrunched up her nose and her lips twisted in concentration.

I had never seen her do that before. Even in the moments after sex when I forced her not to jump out of bed and shut me out, she always had some layer of protection around her. I was assuming this was her—unguarded. She wasn't remembering a practiced answer or carefully choosing her words in an effort to conceal her thoughts.

I had seen many different sides of her over the last few months. I had seen her bitchy, somewhat shy, and incredibly sexy. I had even seen her be kind and thoughtful. Though, I had never not once seen her be cute. And Harper lying next to me with the blush of post fantastic sex still on her cheeks, twisting her lips, and scrunching her nose was off the charts fucking cute.

"We didn't get a chance to. I hadn't really picked one I was planning on keeping yet. I used Aubrey at the truck stop but only because that was the first name that popped into my head. And really, after what happened, I don't want to remember that name."

"What happened at your house? Why didn't you wait for Quinn?" I hated to have to talk about it and upset her, but I had to know. She broke eye contact and started to pull away. "No way. Do not close down and try to hide from me." I wanted to pull her close, but I needed her to come to me—just this once. I don't know why it was important, but it was. "Come here." I rolled onto my back and moved my arm, giving her space to tuck into me.

She did.

Thank fuck.

I kissed the top of her head and waited. After a few beats, she told me what happened, why she had left so suddenly and ditched her phone. As dangerous as it was for her to be without a way to communicate, she had done the smart thing. We didn't know how Russo's men had found her so quickly. Throughout her story, her tone became increasingly flat and detached. Each time her voice cracked, I wished I was the one that was going to end Frankie Russo's miserable life. It wouldn't be long before his reign of terror was over. I hated that Harper was trembling in my arms and I pulled her closer, hugging her to me.

"I left my grandmother's necklace. I had to leave so fast I forgot to get it. Do you think you can take me back to the house and see if it's still there?"

"It's not."

"Oh." Harper's body slumped further into mine.

"I have it, baby. It's in my pocket."

Her head shot off my chest so fast I was thankful for all my years of training and jerked myself back before she could break my nose.

"You have it? You have my grandma's necklace? How?" From the look on Harper's face to the bouncing on the bed in excitement, all that was missing was her clapping her hands and she'd be the perfect image of a six-year-old on Christmas morning.

"Yes, baby."

"Why are you smiling at me like that?"

"Because I like seeing you happy."

Her smile faded and her face gentled. "Thank you."

"I knew what it meant to you. I'm happy I found it."

"Not just for the necklace... for everything."

"Come 'ere." This time I didn't wait for her to come to me. I knifed up, tagged her around the middle, and pulled her into me. "You're welcome."

"How bad was the house?"

"The door was kicked in, but it looked like once they realized you weren't there, they didn't bother with your stuff; they just left."

Harper burrowed further into me. Her arm tightened over my stomach and what was left of the apprehension I didn't know I was holding onto fled.

This.

Harper tucked in tight at my side was what I'd been waiting for. For months, I'd had to force her to allow me to show her any sort of tenderness. Now she gave it freely, and it was better than I could've imagined. The doorbell rang, and she started to jump up.

"Stay."

Her eyes narrowed on me and at the same time she tried to yank her arm away from me. I firmed my grip, keeping her still.

"I'm not a dog."

"Harper," I warned.

"Aiden," she returned.

Goddamn, she was feisty and so fucking sexy when she was pissed.

"You do not ever jump out of our bed. Not ever. But especially when there could be a threat. I get you've been taking care of yourself. And, baby, I'll give it to you, you've done a good job. But now, you're done with that." I loosened my hold and she pulled herself free, rolling off of me. "I'll answer the door. Please stay here. It's probably Roni with food but let me make sure."

I didn't bother waiting for her response as I tagged my pants and pulled them on. I grabbed my shirt and my gun and headed down the hall. I was barely halfway down the stairs before there was knocking at the door, again. A quick check out the window and again through the peephole revealed Roni was getting ready to bang on the door again.

"Damn, you're impatient," I said when I opened the door and stepped aside.

"Well, Reid said you might be occupied and I was to, and I quote, knock until you get unoccupied. So don't blame me, friend. I'm just following orders," she quipped.

Roni flashed a smile and walked past me empty-handed into the living room.

"Nice place. I've never seen this one," Roni commented as she took in the interior of the safe house. "Thank god, Reid didn't try to stick you in the shit hole he calls a cabin."

Reid had a safe house across the Bay Bridge. It was located in the foothills of the Tennessee Valley. Roni was right, it was a shit hole. But the shack had one very valuable feature—a basement. In California, cellars are all but unheard of. The cabin was originally built as a nuclear fallout shelter. Reid mostly used it when he needed privacy when he was trying to obtain information from a person that was being difficult and didn't want to give up the intel they knew.

The last time I was at the cabin was the day I found out that James Kelley had killed my best friend and partner, Jacob Kelley, leaving Ava a widow and JJ without a father. Jimmy was a lowlife drug dealer and gang banger. It was a wonder Jacob and Jimmy were brothers. They were polar opposites. Jacob was everything Jimmy was not. Jimmy and I both entered the basement together. Only one of us came back up that day. I didn't know what Rick and Austin did with his body and I didn't care.

I was fully aware of the crime I was committing in that basement and was prepared to pay the price should I get caught. I had made peace with my decision to end Jimmy's life.

"Let me grab Harper from upstairs."

I took the stairs two at a time and found Harper dressed and standing by the door when I entered the room.

"You okay?" I asked.

"Yeah."

"Then why are you shaking, baby?" I gathered her in my arms and hugged her close.

"Will I ever stop being scared when there is a knock at the door?" she asked.

"Yes. One day this will all be a bad memory," I assured her.

"How can you be so sure?"

"Because I will spend my life making it that way. I'll be by your side every step."

I kissed the top of her head and for the first time Harper broke down. Big racking sobs shook her body and she gave me her weight.

"I... I... can't do this anymore," she cried.

"You don't have to. I'm gonna do it for you. All you have to do is hold on."

12

TAINTED

Harper

After my breakdown yesterday, Mac cleaned me up and took me downstairs to visit with Roni while he brought in the provisions Reid had sent. I'd met Roni and her wife, Melanie, before. Both had come into Del Mar's, sitting at the bar to visit with Ava. I had been introduced and chatted with both of them. But as usual, I didn't connect with either. I had kept my side of the conversation superficial, only talking about the restaurant business. Melanie worked at a trendy café, Pinkcos. It was known around San Francisco for its world-class pancakes.

Yesterday was the first time I had actually taken the time to really speak to Roni. She was funny, smart, and stunning. Melanie and Roni made a beautiful couple. But more than that, they complemented each other perfectly. Roni was a little more reserved; guarded. Probably from working for Reid for so long. She saw the people that Reid investigated and she heard the stories from the men that worked for him. She was tough, and I could see how she could hold her own with the men in Reid's office. Melanie was off-the-chain friendly. She was bubbly and seemed to live her life in the clouds under the careful watch of her wife. I loved that they had that. It kind of reminded me of Ava and Reid. Under Reid's umbrella of protection, Ava had flourished. She was happy—all the time.

Guilt washed over me at the thought of my friend. What Ava must think of me. I had lied to her the whole time I worked for her. I had lied to everyone. The last time I saw her, the look of shock and horror on her face was heartbreaking. I wondered how much Reid had told her about my past. I missed her. JJ and Melody, too.

"What'cha thinking about?" Mac asked as he came up behind me, wrapping his arms around my middle, kissing the top of my shoulder.

Why had I fought this for so long? I never held back when we were in bed together. Not that I ever could. Mac wouldn't allow it. But I'd tried my hardest to fight against his sweet. The soft touches, kisses for no other reason than to be close, the snuggling. I had liked it too much. I liked everything about him and when I was in his arms, I could forget I was Harper Russo—dead girl walking. I could close my eyes and pretend that my life was normal. That I was safe.

But this felt good. Mac behind me, his solid chest pressed close to my back. Strong arms holding me close, wrapping me up in a cocoon of protection.

"Ava," I answered.

His body stiffened just as I knew it would. Silly man still couldn't let the past go.

"What about her?"

"I owe her an apology. Reid, too. I have been lying to all of you. And the day Quinn came to talk to me? I not only fucked up with you, but I hurt her. I feel horrible for all the trouble I caused. She has been nothing but nice to me since I started working at Del Mar's. I hope she'll forgive me."

"She'll understand. I bet she tells you there's nothing to forgive."

I didn't know about that. I didn't think Mac understood how protective Ava was when it came to him. I'd heard the stories about all the women Mac blew through before I met him. Ava was a mama bear when it came to her friend and hated all the women that traipsed through his life. She never thought any of them were good enough for him. Especially after Mac's ex-wife had cheated on him and left him. He never spoke of it. It was like those years didn't exist for him. I didn't think he was holding on to any lingering feelings. He was simply done with that chapter of his life and he'd erased it and moved on. I wish he'd find a way to do that with the guilt he carried about Ava's kidnapping.

"Do you forgive me?" I whispered, afraid of the answer. He'd asked me to trust him but could he ever trust me again? That question had been weighing on my mind since him and Reid had found me in the motel. I wasn't sure he'd ever trusted me in the first place, even before I'd left. Maybe he wanted to, but Mac wasn't stupid; he knew I was keeping secrets. He didn't need to be a detective to read through my lies. That was another reason I'd never made friends, it was too hard to keep up a façade.

Suddenly, I was spun in Mac's arms. Now facing him, he brought his face down eye level with mine.

"As far as I'm concerned, there is nothing to forgive. You didn't lie to be malicious. You were trying to stay alive. Hate to admit this but you were right to be cautious. Quinn taught you well. You did everything you needed to do to protect yourself. Reid gets it. Ava? She'll understand and feel shit that she couldn't have done more for you. No doubt she'll cry and hover around you for a long while. I wouldn't even try to fight her. Let her baby you, it will be easier in the long run."

"Do you think Reid has told her anything?"

"No."

"No? Where does she think he went the other day? Where does she think you are?"

"Baby, first, Ava doesn't know my goings and comings. She doesn't get my schedule and check in on me. She was also married to a cop before Reid. She knows the drill. Reid tells her a lot but shields her where he can. She knows better than to ask him questions when he's on a case. That's not to say he doesn't check in, he does. He just doesn't tell her the specifics."

"Makes sense. I should call her."

"Later. For now, it's important you lie low. No phone calls. Even on the secure phone Reid dropped off. This will be over soon, I promise."

His reminder brought me back to reality. I still had a price tag on my life. What a mess.

"I'm sorry you got sucked into my disastrous life."

"I didn't get sucked in. If I remember correctly, I had to fight tooth and nail to push myself in. You need to stop apologizing and understand I am exactly where I want to be. I'll make you safe; it's just going to take a little more time. After that, no more running, no more hiding. You'll be able to live your life as you should, open and free. There's no way a woman as strong and beautiful as you should be kept locked away from the world. It is a goddamned shame you've had to do it this long."

"Have you always been this sweet?" I asked.

Mac startled, then threw his head back and busted up laughing. He did this for a long time, so long I was getting annoyed.

"Why are you laughing?"

"Because you're hilarious," he told me.

"I don't see how."

"I don't think I've ever been called sweet. Not even as a kid. I'm anything but sweet."

"That's not true. You're sweet to JJ and Melody. You're kind and protective to Ava. And I hate to burst your macho bubble, but you are sweet to me."

"Don't tell JJ you think I'm sweet to him. He's an eleven-year-old boy trying his hand at learning to be a man. Melly is a princess and needs to learn at a young age that she is to be treated as such by any man she comes in contact with. You might see me as being kind to Ava, but she'd disagree. And when the time came, I failed at protecting her." Mac shook his head as if to knock unpleasant thoughts from his mind and continued. "Pleased as fuck if you think I am sweet to you. But, baby, I can promise you my intentions are anything but. They're crude and profane, filthy and arousing. I want to spend my nights loving every inch of you and watch you succumb to my every fantasy. And I want my days filled with the beauty only you can give me. I'm selfish, Harper. I want every part of you. I will take and take until I have it. Your body, your thoughts, your heart. I will settle for nothing less because you already own mine."

"See? Sweet." I trembled, thinking about all the nasty, filthy things Mac had done to my body in the past and at the promise of more.

"Again, pleased you think so," he semi-repeated.

Mac helped me finish putting away the last of the lunch dishes and disappeared into the other room to work. He had spent most of the morning in there. He had a missing person case he was working. I hated to think that my situation was taking his attention away from finding a missing woman. He didn't give me very much information and I didn't ask any questions. I needed to learn Mac would tell me what he could while preserving the integrity of the case.

I padded around the house getting bored. I hated sitting, still preferring to have something to occupy my mind. There was an old saying, *idle hands are the devil's playground.* That was true, only the devil was my brother and his playground was my thoughts. If I sat still too long, memories crept up and threatened to choke me. It was a double-edged sword. Recalling my old life brought highs and the lowest of lows. I could still close my eyes and transport myself back to the stage and the joy I felt when I danced—sautés, jetés, cabrioles, and assemblés. But that memory always faded and morphed into the night my brother relentlessly beat me until I could no longer dance. Those memories are the ones that make me want to hide under my bed and never come out. How could someone be so cruel? Throughout the entire melee, Frankie never used a weapon. He had put his disgusting face near mine and whispered he wanted to feel my bones break under his palms. He used his fists to bloody my face, yelling at me that I would be loyal to the family. In a moment of weakness, I begged him to shoot me and put me out of my misery. He laughed and told me I wasn't worth a bullet. That I needed to die by his hand for my traitorous desertion from the family.

At one point in my life, I was happy, but it was still laced in the ugliness of my family. The money that was used to put me through ballet conservatory was dirty. I might not have known for a hundred percent fact—but I knew enough. I still took it and allowed my father to pay for my apartment in the city. Which was not cheap. I didn't have all the luxuries. No one would've ever looked at me and thought I was a rich socialite, however, I was far from hurting. Most of the girls I knew bunked three or more to an apartment. I had a studio in a trendy part of New York. I didn't have a subway card because my father had always insisted I use cabs. They were safer, he said. After dad died and my brother took over, my bills continued to get paid and my monthly allowance had been raised. Even though I was gainfully employed by a ballet company, I still received what my brother told me was my cut of the pizzeria. The day that stupid pizzeria was ceased by the feds and closed for business was a happy day. That stupid restaurant was the beginning of the end for my family. Dirty business deals and gambling. I later learned that Frankie was also using it to pimp out his stable of girls. Disgusting, low-life pig. I could never be loyal to such a revolting organization. I wished there was a way to magically erase the word mafia from my vocabulary. I never wanted to hear it or say it again. Animals! All of them.

Mac's phone shrilled, and he gently closed the bedroom door he had been using as a workspace.

I wanted to call Ava. I hoped that Mac was right, and she'd understand. However, I'd be happy with her yelling and screaming at me for being a lying bitch as long as in the end, she'd forgive me. I missed her; I missed working at Del Mar's. I even missed the whistling pumpkin pie guy, Kevin. Man, he'd caught a bad deal. Everyone in San Francisco thought he was the serial killer, Simple Simon. Mac and Reid tracked him to his childhood home where he'd lived with a foster family. Mac shot Kevin, luckily not killing him, when they walked into what appeared to be a hostage situation. Kevin had recuperated, even attending Reid and Ava's wedding. His wife, Jane, was a sweetheart. She often came to Del Mar's with him. He always had pumpkin. She had anything *but*. I wondered how Suzie was making out as the new owner? Ava had only turned the keys over to Suzie days before I'd left. After a few small glitches, the sale of the café had been complete. Ava was officially a stay-at-home mom. Well, as stay at home as she wanted to be. Suzie welcomed any hours Ava wanted to give, and Reid was happy with whatever made Ava happy.

I'd never had that. Someone whose only desire was to make sure I was happy. It sounded like that's what Mac was offering, what he wanted. And I didn't know what to do with that. I wasn't sure if I could trust my own feelings. I was afraid that Frankie had crushed more than my legs. What if he'd erased any goodness I had in me? What if I'd always be tainted by my past? Mac said that it didn't matter, but he was a cop. He was good and light. I came from evil and darkness. A family of criminals.

Could I truly open my heart to him and trust him to keep it safe? Hadn't I already done that? I loved him. But... there was always a but... I was waiting for the other shoe to drop. And when it dropped, could I survive the devastation it would bring?

13

SWOON VS SCREAM

Mac

My phone rang with an unknown caller. I shut the door before I picked up, not knowing where Harper was in the house.

"Mac," I answered.

"It's done," Nico Tuscani announced. "Both fronts neutralized. I need a meet. Same place as last time. Eleven tonight."

I wasn't real fond of being summoned, especially by a mob boss, but I had made the deal and Nico had delivered. It was time to pay whatever price he set.

"I'll be there."

Nico didn't respond before he disconnected.

Fuck!

I stabbed at the smooth screen on my phone, dialing Reid.

"Yo." He picked up on the second ring.

"It's done. We have the all clear. I'm taking Harper to my house to get her settled in."

"I heard. Seems all sorts of scumbags are scrambling in Long Island. Word is your friend has mobilized his men to ensure a smooth transition of power. When's your meet?"

Smart fucker. I wasn't going to mention that to Reid. I didn't want him involved in any dealings with the Tuscani family.

"Later. Do you need me to do anything here before we leave?"

"Nope. Lock up and I'll send Roni around later."

I hoped he paid the woman well since she went above and beyond normal secretarial duties. I'd even seen her clean blood out of the guys' clothes before. None of the men that worked for Reid were married. Roni spoiled them, making sure they were taken care of.

"Thanks, brother. I'll call you after I get settled."

"I'll be waiting. Just so we're clear, you're not going in without back-up."

"Appreciate it, but I am. We've been over this. I haven't changed my mind. I made the deal, I pay the price. And you stay clean. Hundred percent."

"We'll see."

My reply was cut off when Reid disconnected. I

wasn't going to budge on this. I knew Reid would have my back and fuck me, there was no one else I'd want in my corner. However, I didn't want him anywhere near this. He had too much to lose. The last thing I wanted was for Ava to lose another husband at the hand of a criminal. If something happened to Reid because I made a deal with a mobster, I was as good as dead. I'd never recover.

I exited the bedroom and found Harper curled up in the same recliner she had been in yesterday.

"How do you feel about blowing this taco joint?" I tried to joke. She seemed lost in her thoughts. I refrained from pushing her to tell me what was weighing so heavy on her mind. The last few days had to have been overwhelming for her.

"Can we? Is it safe?" she asked, sitting up straight.

"It is." I debated how to start the conversation about her living arrangements.

"How do you know?"

"I just do."

Please don't go there.

"Will you tell me?"

She went there. Fuck.

"Do you want to know? I will not lie to you."

She did that cute face scrunch and remained silent. I didn't want to have to tell her; she already had too much shit piled on her plate. I wanted her to breathe easy and let me shoulder the burden of her brother.

"I guess it doesn't matter. If you say I'm safe, I trust you."

"Thank you, baby. Now, I have a favor to ask you."

"Okay." She was still contemplative but had relaxed some. God, I couldn't wait for the day when she was completely at ease. No stress, no folding into herself, no guard up. Just her. Harper.

"I want you to move in with me." I put my finger to her mouth when she went to speak. "I want you in my house. I want to know that you are there. I can't explain why it means so much to me, but it does."

That was a small white lie. I could explain why. I just didn't think she was ready to hear it.

Harper waited for me to drop my hand, then spoke. "Before you shushed me with your finger, I was going to say okay." She tried but failed to scold me in a firm tone. "I still have some stuff at the guesthouse. There's not much. But..." She stopped and ducked her head.

With a hand under her chin, I brought her eyes back to mine. "But, what?"

"It's not a lot and it's not all that nice. But I'm really tired of starting over every time I move. I know it sounds silly, but I don't want to start from scratch again. It's stupid. Never mind. It was junk anyway. I never bought anything nice because I knew I was gonna throw it away as soon as my time was up."

My heart did something weird at the same time my gut tightened. I was conflicted, and I told her as much.

"Baby, I want to simultaneously move all of your belongings into my house and yet, I want to throw them all away. One way, so you're surrounded with your stuff. You never have to run again. I promise you. You'll never have to move and only take what you can fit in a suitcase. However, I want to junk it all so you can surround yourself with nice things. Things you know you can keep. I don't want you to remember the past. I want you only to have peace. I'm fucking torn."

"Thank you for that. Don't worry about the stuff. I think I should start new anyway."

"I packed all your stuff. It's all at my house."

"You did?"

Her eyes rounding in excitement told me she didn't quite mean what she had said.

"I did."

Her face broke out in a wide sexy smile. "Very presumptuous of you."

"I presumed nothing. Honestly? I had hoped I would find you. But if nothing else, having your stuff at my house gave me a measure of you. And at the time, I was willing to take even the smallest sliver. Anything to have you near me."

"See? Sweet! Who knew that big bad Aiden Mackenzie could make a girl swoon?"

So fucking cute, I didn't know what to do with her. I did, however, know one thing; if I didn't hurry up and get her to my house, it would be hours before we left here.

"I don't know about swooning. I'll take your word for it. I do know my skill level is such that I can have you screaming in a matter of seconds. Up you go. Time to get home. I was interrupted last night and didn't get to eat. And, baby, I am fucking starving!" My cock jerked when her face went lazy and her eyes flared. "You are so goddamned beautiful. I am going to tie your ass down and eat you until I get my fill."

"Yes, please," she croaked.

"Come on, let's get you inside."

My jaw clenched, and I bit back my annoyance. Harper's eyes were scanning the area, her body was stiff, and if her shoulders were any higher, they'd be at her ears.

"Hey." Her eyes came to me. "No one is going to hurt you. That's all over for you. I wouldn't have left the house if I wasn't positive."

"Sorry. Habit."

A fucking habit that I was going to break. Fucking Frankie Russo. He had done this to her, made her scared and watchful. That was unacceptable.

I tried really hard to curb my anger as I yanked my keys from the ignition, slammed the car door, stomped around to her side, and jerked the door open. I offered her my hand to help her out and she hesitated. That pissed me off, too.

"I'm sorry," she stammered.

I pulled her from the car and into my arms. "I am not mad at you. You've done nothing wrong. I'm pissed as shit that my woman is scared to get out of my truck in my driveway because her fuckwit brother is a piece of shit. Mark my words, Harper, no more. You breathe easy and live your life. Nothing. I repeat, nothing, touches you from here on out."

"Okay," she whispered, still not believing me.

"You have to trust me."

"I do. Promise."

I led Harper into the house and disarmed the alarm, making a mental note to give her my extra key and show her how the newly upgraded security system worked. Reid had worked his magic and my house was damn near as difficult to breach as Fort Knox. It had cost a mint, but now that Harper would be living here, I was happy with my investment. Even if at the time I thought it was overkill.

I stayed by the door and watched as Harper moved through my living room, taking in the space. I wondered what she thought of it. I bought this house after my divorce. It was in a well-established older neighborhood. One of the few in the city that had a backyard that wasn't the size of a shoebox. It wasn't small by any stretch, but it also wasn't colossal. Three stories, with the whole top floor being one large bonus room. All four sides had huge windows. The view was spectacular, but in the summer, it was hot as shit up there. It was a shame that I rarely used the room.

"This is beautiful," she remarked.

"Thanks."

"I don't know what I was expecting but this certainly wasn't it." Her soft laugh reminded me that I hadn't heard much of it in the past. That was going to change.

"Really? What'd you expect? Take out cartons and beer bottles?"

"No. Maybe. I mean, you're a little old to be living in a frat house." She giggled again, and my gut tightened. "I didn't think it would be so well decorated. It looks like it has a woman's touch." She paused and looked at the large built-it bookcase that took up the entire back wall of the room. "You even have framed pictures and knick-knacks on the shelves."

"No woman has ever been in this house," I told her. "I put those there."

"Really?" She sounded shocked.

"Why was coming to my house a hard limit for you?" I asked, realizing the truth in my statement. Not even Harper had been to my place in the over nine months we'd been seeing each other. At first, I thought it was a smart move on her part—a safety precaution. However, as the months went by, even after she got to know me, she still wouldn't agree.

"Because seeing where you lived, being in your space, was too personal for me. Silly I know, especially considering all that we've done." Her cheeks flushed a pretty pink. "And being here now, seeing your furniture, your books, imagining you sitting on your couch drinking a beer and watching a game. I know that I was right to stay away."

"Why's that?"

"I was already having a hard time not getting too attached to you, even before you saw me at Stripes and we started a physical relationship. Seeing you at the café, watching you talk and laugh with Reid, how gentle you were with Ava. As hard as I tried not to pay attention, to ignore the pang of jealousy I felt when you smiled at other women, or I heard you talk about them, it was there. I couldn't have you, but I still wanted your attention. After we started seeing each other, I knew that if I saw your place, saw a personal, intimate side of you, I'd never be able to leave when the time came."

Holy shit. I had no idea that she'd felt that way. She'd never shown a bit of interest in me. All the times Reid and I sat at the counter at Del Mar's grabbing a cup of coffee, shooting the shit, she had gone to great lengths to avoid me, or so it seemed. She'd been a mystery to me. No other woman had ever blown me off the way she had when I first met her. She was like the arctic—cold and unyielding.

"Me coming to your house wasn't too personal?" I asked.

"No. The guesthouse wasn't mine. Sure, I had some personal items there, but they were generic. There was nothing in that place that was really me. It sounds silly, but I never thought of that place as home. It was a stop. Another place to sleep before I took off again."

Jesus. I couldn't imagine what her life had been like. Never settling, never having anything that was hers—not even a name. Stopping and starting. Never truly living.

"I'm glad you're here, Harper."

"Me, too." Her smile lit up my living room and my heart in a way I never thought possible. She was here and I was never letting her go.

NOT EVER

Harper

Mac showed me around the rest of his house. The more I saw, the more embarrassed I became. I was twenty-nine years old and had nothing to show for my life. I didn't own a home, furniture, a car. Hell, I didn't even own a proper wardrobe or coffee maker. I had nothing. The clothes on my back and a backpack. That's how I'd lived my life for the last two years. It was hard to wrap my head around the fact that at one time I was normal. I was like any other person living life and now I couldn't even remember what *normal* felt like.

I could see the frustration in Mac. He said he wasn't mad at me, but I still felt like shit. I trusted him at his word. If he said I was no longer in danger, I believed him. As much as I wanted to know what he'd done to ensure my safety, I refrained from asking for the details. I couldn't handle them, not now. Ignorance was bliss, and I just wanted to be ignorant for a change. I was so damn tired of thinking, of looking over my shoulder every five seconds, of watching the world pass me by. I knew it was stupid, I should've told him I wanted him to tell me—he would've. But I wanted the peace he offered. I wasn't going to look a gift horse in the mouth. If it turned out to be the wrong choice, I would deal with it later.

My life was so screwed up, it couldn't get much worse.

Mac had disappeared into the kitchen, leaving me to explore on my own. I loved that he had pictures of Reid, Ava, JJ, and Melly displayed. There was a photo collage of Mac and JJ, JJ and Melly, Mac and Reid, Reid and Ava, all pictures from Reid and Ava's wedding. That had been a beautiful day. Perfect weather, great company, and a stunning backdrop as we cruised on the *Sea-duction*. My heart seized when I came across a photo of me and Mac from the wedding. We were on the dance floor, Mac was holding me close, and it was in profile. I was laughing at Ava, who I knew even though it was not shown in the picture, had been dancing beside us with Blaze. A beautiful woman in a white wedding gown dancing with a ginormous biker full of tats. The image had struck me as hilarious and both Ava and I had burst out laughing. In the photograph, Mac was staring at me with a small smile ghosting his handsome face.

I remember that day. I remember the ache I felt at the realization I would never have that. Not the wedding. Not the man.

"You looked so beautiful that day," Mac said, coming up behind me.

"Thank you." I always felt shy when Mac complimented me even though he did it often. He was forever telling me I was perfect or beautiful. It was hard not to believe him when he said those things to me. "You didn't look too bad yourself."

"That's my favorite picture of the bunch."

I didn't believe that. But it was nice of him to say. There was no way it was his favorite. Not with the abundance of pictures of his godson JJ in all stages of his life. I noticed there were pictures of him and Jacob, too. I picked one up and studied it closely.

"That was taken a year before Jacob died. We had all gone camping. That was the year that JJ caught his first fish. He was so little that Jacob had to help him reel it in."

"What a great memory," I whispered.

I had seen plenty of pictures of Jacob displayed at Ava and Reid's house. I was taken aback at first. Pictures of a deceased husband on the same shelf as the current husband struck me as odd. However, after Ava had explained that Reid had been the one to demand that Jacob be displayed, my respect for Reid grew.

"He was a great friend. I miss him."

I turned in Mac's arms to face him. I didn't like how his tone had changed. It wasn't one of pain but of guilt. I hated that for him. I knew the story of Jacob's murder. I had also been around long enough to know Mac shouldered a lot of guilt.

"If you ever want to talk about him, I'm here to listen."

He brushed his lips against my forehead and said, "Thanks, baby." Closing down any conversation about Jacob.

I wasn't going to push. Not now. However, it was a subject that needed to be aired out.

"You ready to see the upstairs?" Mac leaned in and whispered in my ear. I couldn't control my reaction. I never could when Mac's tone became rumbly and seductive. He chuckled when I shivered at his suggestion. "I hope you're ready." He stopped speaking long enough to touch the silver at my throat. "I want you naked on your knees." His hand moved from my collar to the nape of my neck and squeezed. "After I take my fill of your mouth, I'm going to cuff you and fuck you. First with my tongue, then my fingers, and after that I'm gonna give you my cock."

"Yes, Sir."

I wasn't sure why I had said yes. He hadn't really asked a question, but my insides were a mess and I couldn't think straight. My belly had a million butterflies dancing, my panties were soaked, and my mind was doing cartwheels.

"Good girl. First door on your right. Go on up and get ready for me. I need to get a few things."

With a swat to my ass, he sent me up the stairs. I found the first door on the right, quickly stripped out of my clothes, and tossed them into the laundry hamper Mac had in the corner.

My knees sank into the plush carpet and my body relaxed. With my hands clasped behind my back, I lowered my head and my breathing evened out. Mac's bare feet came into focus and I was at peace.

"So beautiful. Thank you."

He always thanked me.

I remained quiet.

"Where are you, my sweet girl?"

"Green, Master."

I heard the swift intake of breath and wished I could see his face. I had never called him Master. I didn't know why the word slipped from my mouth. Sir, seemed... not enough. Sir had been what I called Mac when I was trying to hold myself apart from him.

"Eyes," he growled, and I immediately obeyed.

I was wrong. I didn't want to see his face. I wasn't sure what was swirling behind his eyes; however, there was only a tiny sliver of blue left.

"I've changed my mind. I am not going to fuck you." My heart sank. I'd messed up. I should've known better than to call him *Master* until we'd discussed it. "We're past fucking, little one. I'm going to love you until you lose yourself. Worship you until you're breathless. I'm going to irrevocably bind you to me—there is no going back. Not now, not ever."

I choked down the lump in my throat. I desperately wanted to jump up and pepper his face with a thousand kisses and tell him that no sweeter words had ever been said by anyone—ever. I wanted him to know I felt that same way. But I didn't. I gave him something better.

"Yes, Master."

"Open," he demanded.

The top button popped.

The zipper was drawn down.

My mouth opened.

***

"I'm so sorry I lied to you."

After Mac had made good on all his promises and then some, we cleaned up, made dinner, and he told me I had the all-clear to call Ava. I didn't delay. The first few minutes on the phone were tense and I thought she was going to hang up on me. I couldn't blame her, but it hurt, only solidifying my resolve to patch things up. I asked her to come to Mac's house and talk to me. I thought if she could see Mac and I together, it might soften her up.

When she'd stomped in the door, I thought I had made a mistake. She didn't look softened up; she looked like a pissed-off mama bear ready to claw my eyes out. Reid came in after her with JJ and Melody. I relaxed a little knowing Ava wouldn't commit aggravated assault in front of her children.

Mac told the kids to go up to the third floor and watch TV while he and Reid disappeared into Mac's office to "work". With a chuckle and a kiss to my forehead, Mac left me alone in the living room with Ava.

I didn't delay.

I spilled my guts.

I told her about growing up, attending dance conservatory, my time with the ballet company, my brother, the murders I had witnessed, my beating, waking up in the hospital, Quinn, as much as I could remember about the places I had been while on the run. I told her everything. I rushed it out as fast as I could, not wanting to linger and dwell on any of it. It was easier to tell the story as if I was a bystander rather than it being my life.

When I was done, we were both crying. Other than the breakdown with Mac the other day, I hadn't cried since the day I was released from the hospital. I had bottled it all up and locked it away.

"I'm the one that's sorry," Ava started. "I'm sorry you had to go through all of that alone. I'm sorry you couldn't confide in me or ask Mac and Reid for help."

"I didn't want to put anyone in danger. My brother's a monster."

"Still. I wish we could've helped you. How did Mac... I don't know... fix everything?"

"I didn't ask."

I waited for her to tell me how stupid I was for not inquiring about what he had done to make my brother call off the hit but instead she shocked me.

"That's smart. I've learned not to ask questions I don't want the answers to."

"You think? You don't think I'm crazy?"

"If Mac says you're safe, you're safe. There's no reason to worry yourself with the details."

I was relieved she agreed with me. It might've been a copout, but I was willing to run with it.

"So... Harper, huh? I never thought you looked like a Laura." Ava laughed.

"Really?"

"Yeah. Should I call you Harper now? Are you staying with Laura? Or are you picking a new name?" she asked.

"I haven't had time to give it much thought."

And I hadn't. Mac had also asked but then he dazzled me with his serious sexual expertise and made me forget. He was good at that—making the world fall away until all that was left was him. My world narrowed when I was with Mac and that was perfectly okay with me.

"Well, now you're free to be whoever you want to be."

I was dumbfounded as her words hit me; it was like I'd been struck by a two by four. Before I understood what was happening, Mac was picking me up off the couch and settling me on his lap. "Baby? What's wrong?" He wiped the moisture from my cheeks and held tight.

When did he come into the room?

"I don't... I've... I've never been free." I barely got the words out. "I don't know who I even am anymore."

"Sweet, strong, Harper. You can be anything you want to be. But you don't need to decide now. Take some time and just relax," Mac whispered into my hair.

I didn't answer. I just melted into Mac and tried to soak up every bit of warmth he offered.

15

SAVOR

Mac

I told Harper while we were eating I was going to run out later that night for work. She said she was fine being at the house alone; we'd gone over the alarm and she had a new cell phone. But now that it was time for me to leave to go meet Nico, I was having second thoughts about leaving her at the house by herself. As much as I wanted to get this shit over with, she was more important. I could've called Reid or canceled with Nico altogether and just when I was going to suggest Reid come back over, Harper squeezed my hand, bringing my attention to her.

"I'm fine. I promise. I'm in bed and exhausted. I'll be asleep in five minutes." She yawned.

Shit.

"I'll be back as fast as I can. This shouldn't take more than an hour."

"Be safe." She smiled and snuggled into her pillow.

I straightened and took in the sight. Harper Russo in our bed, naked, shiny blonde hair fanned over the pillow, her features soft and relaxed, and a strikingly beautiful smile on her puffy well-kissed lips.

Stunning.

Perfect.

Mine.

Seeing her like this, I knew that every moment that had led to this was worth it.

"I love you," I blurted out, without thinking of the consequences.

Scratch that. I knew the consequences. At that moment, I couldn't have cared less about the repercussions. I couldn't hold the words back any longer. I couldn't. I didn't want to.

"You do?" she asked, pulling herself up on an elbow.

"I do. I love you, Harper."

If I'd thought Harper lying in my bed smiling up at me was perfect—I was wrong. Because Harper in my bed up on an elbow smiling at me so wide after I'd told her I loved her, I thought my heart was going to explode. That was fucking perfect.

"I love you, too, Mac."

A stillness washed over me. Tranquility I had never known rooted deep down in a place that had always been cynical and in constant unrest. I was amazed how saying three words out loud could change everything.

I wanted to stand here all night and savor the moment we'd shared, but the sooner I left, the sooner I'd be back.

"I wish I could crawl in bed and show you how much those words mean to me. Undoubtedly, I'll fail, because there's no way I could ever repay what you just gave me. It shits me to say this, but I have to go take this meeting. When I get back, I'm gonna spend the rest of the night trying."

"Promise?"

"Promise."

"Be safe and hurry home."

Fuck, but that felt good.

I WALKED into Nonna Maria's and much like the first time my stomach knotted. Nico and his man were sitting in the same place in the back of the empty restaurant.

I moved to the table and took a seat across from them.

"I trust your woman is well." Nico broke the silence and I narrowed my eyes. I didn't want him thinking about Harper. "I was warned you keep a loose leash on your temper. By the daggers you are shooting my way, it seems I was well informed."

"You were," I confirmed.

"Frankie has been taken care of."

I remained quiet. It seemed he wanted to repeat what he'd already told me over the phone.

"The hit has been called off. I've also put the word out that Harper Russo is under my protection."

"The fuck?" I bit out, and Branson sat up straight, cutting his stare to me. "That was not part of the deal."

Nico's hand went to Branson's shoulder, giving him a hard slap before the big man settled back into his chair.

"It is a necessary precaution. There are some in New York that are not happy at her reprieve. Whatever her reasons, however as much you might agree with her, she broke the code of silence. *The Omertá.* There are some that think just because the Russo family no longer exists that she still should pay for her crimes. We live in a world that demands certain loyalties. Truth be told, Frankie Russo was a bottom feeder piece of shit. He ran his family like he ran his pizzeria. He had no foresight, no finesse, and he was morally bankrupt."

"And you?" I cut him off. "Are you morally bankrupt?"

Nico threw his head back and busted out laughing.

"Perhaps. Most people would say I am. However, I don't demand loyalty. I earn it." Nico leaned forward and steepled his fingers. "Make no mistake, if you fuck with me I'm a cold-blooded vindictive son-of-a-bitch. But I reward faithfulness. I also honor my word. I gave you my word I would take care of Harper's problem. I've done just that, and I will continue to do so until I feel like it's no longer needed."

"And the price?"

There was no sense sugar-coating the true intent of this meeting. We weren't two friends knocking back a few drinks and shooting the shit. Nico wanted to lay out the terms of payment.

"Less than you owe me."

"Care to elaborate?"

"A simple turn of your head. I'm entertaining a young woman. Her father isn't *happy* she is in my company. However, she will remain in my care until certain debts are paid."

Fuck.

"Nicole Brown."

Goddamn it all to hell.

"Let's keep names out of it," he said.

Mother fucker. I didn't need him to confirm her

name. Nico Tuscani had kidnapped the police chief's daughter.

"Fuck."

All three of us remained quiet as I ran through different scenarios. Nico had given me the confirmation I needed that Tom Brown was dirty. And Nicole was going to pay for her father's crimes. My gut turned at the thought of Nicole suffering the same fate as Harper. Beaten and bloodied.

Of course, I could walk into the station, turn in my shield, admit to hiring Nico to kill Frankie, and turn Nico in before he killed Nicole. I could live with paying for my crimes more than I could live with the knowledge I allowed Nicole to die.

As if sensing my internal struggle, he said, "She is unharmed and will remain that way. I'm not a fucking animal. I have no interest in hurting some innocent woman just because her father is a lying sack of shit."

"I'm the lead investigator on the case. Brown handed me the case personally. I assume because he knows my ties to Logan Reid and Blaze."

"That may be true. Brown might be a bastard, but he's a smart one. I'm sure he thinks at the end of this he can buy you off. Make no mistake, Brown knows where his daughter is."

"Be that as it may, I have to investigate her disappearance. If I don't, red flags will be thrown up all over the place."

"Due diligence, I get it. Investigate. I'm not telling you not to look into her disappearance. All I am asking is you look the other way if anything points in my direction. Better yet, you should look into why it's pointing at me. You might find all the answers you're looking for. The politician fucks like to call me a criminal. They're not wrong, but at least I don't lie about who I am. I don't wait until someone's back is turned so I can sink my knife in their back. I do that shit face-to-face. I don't pretend to be a *friend*."

My jaw ached from clenching my teeth so hard. This was so fucked. Reid was right—Nico owned me. I wasn't sure if I could live with this mark on my soul. The way he said friend gave me pause. Was he talking about Blaze? I didn't like the insinuation, but I was unwilling to ask for clarification. Not that I thought Nico would tell me the truth, anyway.

"And your end game? Where does the girl end up?"

"That's up to her father."

Harper. This was for Harper, I reminded myself.

It did nothing to ease the knot.

16

KNITTING

Harper

"It's too soon."

"No, it's not. I'm bored sitting at home. You're at work all day. I've unpacked what I'm keeping and trashed everything else," I reminded Mac.

I had gone through the boxes that Mac had packed from the guesthouse and put away everything I wanted. My heart was brimming with excitement when I hung my clothes up in Mac's big walk-in closet and placed the few books I owned next to his on his built-in bookshelf. It was silly, but for the first time in years, I was unpacking. Truly and really settling in. I wasn't worried about having to throw what I needed in a backpack and take off at a moment's notice. I had even gone to the mall and bought towels. Big, fluffy, extra-large, plush white towels and replaced Mac's ratty ones in his bathroom. I also got a soap dispenser, toothbrush holder, and bath mats. I was so happy to be doing something as normal as shopping with a friend I wasn't fazed when Mac argued with me about spending money. It wasn't the amount I had spent that he was mad about; it was the fact that I was using mine. I'd refused to use the credit card he'd left. I also wouldn't take the cash he tried to give me to pay me back for all the stuff I bought. Now that I wasn't running, I had money to spend. It wasn't a lot, but I could afford to buy what I wanted for the house. Undeterred, he'd stood in the doorway of the bathroom with his arms crossed. Stubborn. But then so was I. I'd stood in the bathroom, hands on my hips, mirroring his macho posture, and commenced throwing him attitude.

I wasn't giving in and to my total amazement, Mac relented.

Sort of.

We'd come to a compromise. I wouldn't argue or offer to pay the household bills and mortgage and he wouldn't complain when I bought groceries and stuff for the house. Which was a good thing because he'd yet to see the new comforter and sheets I'd bought for his bed. They'd cost a mint but were well worth it. Pure luxury. In the last few years, I'd bought cheap scratchy bedding, not wanting to waste money on something I knew I'd have to throw away. Now that I was staying and putting down roots, I was going all out.

When Mac had asked me to move in with him, for about two seconds, I thought about telling him no. Maybe it wasn't such a good idea rushing and moving in with him. Then I realized I was done putting my life on hold. I wasn't going to waste another minute. If Mac wanted me to live with him, why should I say no? Why shouldn't I have something I wanted? I decided to say fuck it and jump. That's what I was going to do from now on. Jumping. No more thinking, calculating every risk, my every move, looking over my shoulder, waiting for someone to kill me. Mac had said I was done living that life and I agreed.

I was done.

I wanted Mac. I wanted to live with him. I wanted normal. I desperately wanted the happiness he promised.

I was taking it.

So here I was standing behind the counter at Del Mar's serving Mac and Reid their morning coffee, being normal. Mac, for his part, had tried to talk me out of going back to work. He had tried convincing me into the early morning hours that I didn't need to work. He used every tool in his extensive arsenal to exhaust me so I'd call Suzie and tell her I wasn't coming in. While I enjoyed every second of his idea of sexual persuasion and only got two hours of sleep, I still drug my ass out of bed this morning.

"So get a hobby. Maybe learn how to knit or better yet, summer's coming, you can work in the yard," Mac suggested.

"You didn't just say that." I leaned over the counter, coming closer to Mac. "Please tell me you didn't just tell me to start knitting."

"Oh, boy." This came from Reid.

"Okay. Maybe not knitting. But there's plenty of stuff you can do around the house."

"Oh, shit." That was from Ava who had now joined the fray.

"So this is how it's going to be? You want a house bunny to stay at home and cook and clean for you? Is that it, Mac?"

If I'd been smart, I would've stopped after *house bunny* when his eyes narrowed on me. Mac was pissed. Well, I was, too. I wasn't going to sit around the house and take advantage of Mac.

"Harper," Mac warned.

"Aiden."

Now would've been a really good time to shut my mouth.

"The fact that you'd say I want you to stay home and cook for me is jacked. You're my woman, not my maid." Mac stopped and pushed closer. With me leaning over the counter and him inching forward, we were almost nose to nose. "You have spent years running. Stressed, tired, and scared. Is it too fucking much to want my woman to relax and live easy for a while before she goes back to work? I don't give a rat's ass if you stay home and watch afternoon talk shows all day. I don't care if you stay in bed and read. I really don't care if you take a bubble bath and eat fucking ice cream all day. What I do care about is that you unwind and rest."

"Well, damn," Ava muttered, pulling my attention to her.

I felt like shit for saying something so foolish to Mac. I knew him better than that. He'd never suggested I stay home and be his maid. I hadn't thought of it that way when I said it.

"Sorry."

"If you're sorry, then come here and give me a kiss so my stubborn ass woman can get to work." I closed the distance and brushed my lips against his. Unfortunately, it was a soft chaste kiss appropriate for the mixed company we were in. When I pulled back, he said, "Please think about only working part-time for a while. I know you'd go crazy sitting around the house for too long. But I really would like you to be able to take some time for yourself."

"I'll think about it and talk to Suzie." I compromised. It was hard not to when Mac's reasons for me working minimal hours were heartfelt. He'd been open and honest with me; he deserved the same from me.

"Thanks, Aiden."

"Fuck me. About damn time," Reid chimed in. "Ava baby, can I get a refill please?"

Ava didn't answer. Not verbally anyway. She smiled at her husband and threw in a flirty wink as she walked away to grab the coffee pot.

"I have tables to check on."

I didn't give Mac a wink, but I did give him what I hoped was a flirtatious smile and went about checking my tables.

The early morning crowd at Del Mar's was eclectic. Businessmen and women in suits and ties. College students with their laptops open, fingers flying over their keyboards. Police officers and paramedics. You never knew what the morning rush would bring. When Ava opened Del Mar's after Jacob was killed, the café became a regular spot for San Francisco's first responders. They'd come out in droves to support the widow of a fallen officer. All these years later, they still came in. Before shift, after shift, or when they got a moment to eat a quick meal between calls. Everyone who came into Del Mar's understood that the men and women in blue got served first. Not because they were better than anyone else, but they could be called away at a moment's notice.

"Order up, Laura... I mean... Harper," Suzie said when I shouldered through the swinging doors separating the dining room from the kitchen.

I couldn't help it, I laughed, and Suzie frowned. "Sorry, Suz. I don't care what name you use. I know it's confusing."

"I've always known you as Laura but I kinda like Harper better. It fits you. It's just gonna take a little time."

Suzie looked like she had something else on her mind. Her frown deepened, and she busied herself with arranging plates on a tray.

"What's wrong?" I asked.

"Nothing's wrong."

"Bullshit, babe. I've worked with you awhile now. Something is wrong. Do you, um, not want me coming back to work?"

Shit. I hadn't thought that maybe Suzie and her husband Michael wouldn't want me working here anymore after I told them the truth. Ava was happy I was back at the café, but Ava didn't own Del Mar's anymore.

"What? No. I mean, yes. Yes, I want you here working." She pushed some more plates around and avoided looking at me. "I heard what Mac said. I wasn't trying to eavesdrop or anything, but maybe he's right. I don't want to be selfish and put you back on the schedule too soon. You're my best server and I can use you as many hours as you're willing to work."

"You're not being selfish. I love working here. I'm not going anywhere. I told Mac I'd talk to you about only working part-time for a while. But, Suzie, I don't want to jam you up. This is a business and you have to staff it. If you need me full-time, I'm ready. I promise."

She stopped fiddling with her tray and snapped her eyes to mine with a ferocity I didn't understand.

"No! You take the part-time shift. You and I both have a firsthand understanding of how precious life is. How fast your world can change. You've been living a half-life for so long you need to take time and enjoy all the things you lost while you had to hide."

Suzie did understand. The crazy man, Carl, who had stalked Ava, had beaten Suzie almost to death in an effort to get to Ava. Thankfully, Reid's guys had gone to the café after closing to pick up the nightly deposit and they had found Suzie in the nick of time. Unfortunately, when everyone had rushed to Suzie's aid, Reid had unwittingly fallen into a trap. Carl found Ava and killed Rick, the man that Reid had left to protect her. That night was a tragedy all the way around. Rick died. Suzie was near dead. JJ was scared to death hiding under the bed, listening to his mother scream in fear. And Ava was taken. All the men were beside themselves, and that was putting it mildly. Reid went ballistic, Mac not far behind that, and Michael, Suzie's husband, had to be locked down at the hospital.

"I'm sorry I couldn't visit you while you were in the hospital."

Now was not the time to have this conversation; it was too emotional. But I needed her to know how sorry I was. I couldn't bring myself to see Suzie beaten and almost dead. It was too close to home.

"Don't you apologize for that." She waved her hand in front of her face. "We'll save that conversation for a bottle of wine and a box of Kleenex." She turned to pick up her tray. "Part-time it is, Harper."

With practiced ease, she lifted her tray and balanced it on her palm while she pushed the doors open and disappeared.

Yea. Part-time. That would be perfect. I would have time to do nothing and still keep busy working a few hours a day. And while I wouldn't admit this to Mac, his yard looked like shit and could use a total overhaul. I had never tended to a garden, yet I was ecstatic at the thought of working in his. Totally normal!

I delivered my food, refilled drinks, and stopped at a table with two haggard looking paramedics. Both were in uniform and looking beat. I wasn't sure if they were coming off a long overnight shift or just going in. With all the unrest going on in the city, it could've gone either way.

Mac turned off the news last night after spitting out a few colorful expletives at the newscaster when she speculated about Chief Brown's daughter and the police department's lack of control of the protestors. One had nothing to do with the other, but the newscaster had made sure to throw in a dig where she could. I had never met Nicole Brown and it was sad that a woman was missing but completely irresponsible to report her disappearance the way the news was. Not to mention disrespectful. A little girl had been killed and the public was outraged as we all should've been. But the police couldn't stop the peaceful protest; they had to stand by and wait until it turned ugly. And they didn't have to wait long, the crowds were becoming more and more dangerous. Protests were turning into riots. Mac was diligently investigating Nicole's disappearance while his fellow officers tried to protect the public.

"Here you go." I smiled and dropped two to-go cups along with the check.

"Thank you," the woman replied.

I looked at the name tape on her uniform, Galloway. A quick check of the man sitting across from her revealed his name was Myers. He reached for the check, but Galloway shook her head and snatched it before he could pick it up.

"My turn. You bought last shift. And lunch the time before that."

"We're keeping track now?" Myers laughed but didn't stop her from taking the check.

I cleared off the plates and smiled at their easy camaraderie. I missed that. I wanted that. For so long I had held myself apart from everybody who had tried to befriend me. I didn't have to do that anymore. Mac had given me the best gift anyone ever could—freedom.

"No. But you can't buy three times in a row..." Galloway started when I turned my back and left the table.

"Harper," Mac called when I walked by the counter.

I placed my load of dirty dishes in the bus tub and wiped my hands before I moved to his side. As soon as I did, his cologne invaded my senses. I loved the way he smelled; intense, sensual, fresh. The fragrance mixed with his natural scent brought back memories of last night. Maybe part-time wouldn't be so bad after all. There would be no way I could keep up all-night sexcapades and still wake up for the morning shift. Now that I had a choice, I'd gladly give up the morning shift and enjoy Mac's stamina. He'd always taken his time drawing out my pleasure, but since I'd moved in, something had changed. He was still just as attentive but there was a new urgency behind his touch. I loved it.

Mac reached out and pulled me into him. "Gotta go to work, baby. Call me when you're done and we'll figure out getting you a ride home."

"Okay."

"Have a good day." He kissed my forehead and gave me a swat on my butt.

"You, too. Be safe."

"Always."

He picked up his coffee off the counter and with a wave over his shoulder he was gone.

So normal.

17
─────

GRAHAM CARTWRIGHT

Mac

I hated leaving Harper at Del Mar's but I had work to do and Blaze had called late last night asking me to stop by the clubhouse.

I skirted a thin line with Iron Claw MC. Reid, too. His brother Damion was the president of the club for years. He was murdered last year and Blaze took over as president. I liked Damion and Blaze both, but our friendship was precarious at best. Blaze didn't edge the line of the law—his club was miles away from it. But I respected Blaze; he took care of his club and family and did his best never to let his dealings bleed into Reid's life. And never had he ever asked me for a marker or asked me to help him break the law. I appreciated that; Reid did as well.

I pulled into the forecourt and parked. Blaze was

outside with a few guys gathered around a Harley, all proudly displaying their Iron Claw colors. The men all straightened when they heard my truck door slam. Two men broke from the huddle and headed toward the clubhouse. The top rocker of their leather cuts read prospect, meaning they weren't fully patched members; therefore, Blaze wouldn't discuss club business in front of them.

Fuck.

I had a pretty good idea why Blaze had called me for a meet. The same reason I was getting ready to visit one of his members in lockup after I left here. I didn't want to have this conversation with Blaze—at all.

"Mac," Blaze billowed as I approached.

"Yo," I returned.

I noticed Blaze had dismissed his other men with a tilt of his chin. He waited until they were out of earshot before he continued. It wasn't good business for the president of an outlaw one percenter motorcycle club to be talking to a cop.

"I take it you've heard." Blaze crossed his ginormous tattooed arms over his chest.

"I have. I've seen the video as well," I confirmed.

"It's fucking bullshit."

Fuck me. I really didn't want to discuss this with Blaze.

"Doesn't look that way, brother. The video is clear.

Riggers lit the Molotov cocktail and torched a cruiser. There is no way to deny that. The problem is Nicole Brown was last seen standing by that same police cruiser. The video cuts off as Riggers is approaching the car. Nicole Brown hasn't been seen since."

The video I was referencing was cell phone footage that had been put on the internet of a vigil that had turned into an out and out riot. And Riggers was a patched member of Iron Claw. I had to admit the video was damning, and I didn't like that Riggers, and by extension Blaze, was involved.

"Mother fucking piece of shit. Riggers is being set up."

"Care to tell me how you know that?"

Blaze's face lit red and if I didn't already know how the man had received his road name, I would've guessed it was because his eyes ignited when he was angry.

"You sure you want me to tell you."

Fuck me.

"Will it incriminate you?"

Blaze didn't answer. He held my eyes and told me everything I needed to know.

I took what I had hoped was a deep cleansing breath and slowly blew it out. It wasn't enough; the pressure that had begun behind my eyes was still puls-ing, the promise of a headache was imminent.

Between Nico and now Blaze's involvement, nothing good was going to come from my investigation. I was so screwed.

"Riggers is being held on assault and the attempted murder of the district attorney's assistant. Not on kidnapping charges. As it stands, Riggers will be questioned as a witness."

"That Mother fucker."

"Who?"

"Graham Cartwright," Blaze spit out.

I had known Blaze a long time. He had a bad temper and had no issue showing it off. However, Blaze was smart. A clever fucker that most underestimated because he was a biker. He also played his cards close to his vest. Blaze answering me with a name was telling.

"The district attorney. I take it you're not a fan." Blaze didn't find my comment amusing and narrowed his eyes on me. It was easy to see how he intimidated his enemies, his scowl was downright ugly. "Straight up, Blaze. You have never put me in a situation where I was uncomfortable, and I've never lied to you. I'd like to think we have a mutual understanding. But I'm gonna ask you this, off the record. I take what you say to the grave. If you have something on the DA, I need to know about it."

"I have more dirt on that Mother fucker than you

have hours in the day. Most of it will fuck me and the club over if it were to come out. I wouldn't ask you to keep that and, brother, I respect you and I *trust* you. But the secrets I keep aren't mine. They're Iron Claw's and I hope you understand but those go with *me* to the grave."

Sweet mother of God.

"Is Cartwright in bed with Chief Brown?"

"Goddamned right he is," Blazed answered, not the least bit surprised I knew the PC was dirty.

"Fuck."

"Fuck is right. Cartwright is greedy. Greedy men are almost as bad as a man that's desperate. They fuck up. They don't think things through and make bad plays. Cartwright fucked up. He's trying to play a game and he's so far out of his league it's not even funny. That dickweed is about to get burned."

I needed to put the brakes on Blaze disposing of Cartwright.

"Can I ask that you hold off settling any disputes with Cartwright until after I finish my investigation?"

Blaze threw his head back and what I think was supposed to be a laugh came out gravely and menacing.

"Listen to you, trying to sound all official. If you're asking me not to put that Mother fucker to ground, I'll give you two weeks. After that, all bets are off, Mac. And I'll repeat, I respect you, but I won't give two fucks if your investigation is over. Cartwright fucked with my club, he fucked with a patched member, and there is retribution to be paid. And brother Cartwright will be paying."

Goddamn. Blaze all but admitted he was planning on assassinating the district attorney and I was going to look the other way.

"'Preciate it."

"Don't mention it."

"How's the kid?"

"Fucking perfect. Nina's happy. So I'm happy."

Fatherhood looked good on Blaze. When I mentioned his son, his entire body relaxed and his face softened. Seemed the big-ass-scary biker had a soft spot after all.

"Glad to hear it. I'm out. See ya around."

"Yeah, see ya."

ON THE RIDE out to the prison where Riggers was being held, I called Reid and filled him in on what Blaze had told me. Reid, being in the private sector, had more leeway than I did. He and Blaze also had a bond that I did not have with the man. Reid would step in and protect his brother's club where he could.

I checked in my weapon with the desk sergeant

and was buzzed back into the inner walls of the prison and shown to an interrogation room.

"Cameras are to be off as well as any listening devices," I told the officer that had escorted me.

"Standard procedure..." I cut the officer off with a gesture of my hand.

"I don't care what your standard procedure is. If you have an issue, call Chief Brown."

The officer nodded and pushed open the door.

"He's on his way down now." With that, the officer left, leaving me alone in the small white room. I checked the corner, happy when there was not a blinking red light indicating the room was being watched.

In walked Riggers, orange inmate jumpsuit, plastic slip-on shower shoes over white socks, hands cuffed in front of his large frame. When I got to his face, I had to do a double take. He'd been worked over pretty good. Black eye, bruising on his cheek, and a cut lip. He was fucked up.

The officer shoved Riggers farther in the room and Riggers clenched his jaw as he stumbled forward, no doubt biting back the urge to knock the officer out for daring to put his hands on him. On the streets, no one would think to touch Riggers, let alone shove him like a punk.

I sat across from Riggers and waited for the door to click shut before I spoke.

"Who did that to your face?" I started.

"Like you fucking care."

"Let me be the judge of what I care about," I returned.

Riggers remained silent and leaned back in his chair.

"You know who I am?"

This would go much easier if Riggers knew my connection to Blaze.

"Yep," he confirmed.

"So you know I fucking care who did that to your face. You got issues with other inmates, not my problem. You're a grown ass man, I assume you can handle yourself. Now, if a guard in here is jacking you around? I got issues with that."

"What you gonna do, officer? Put me in protective custody and cuddle me at night?"

Goddamn, why do people have to be so fucking difficult?

"What do you know about Nicole Brown?"

Riggers' eyes flared before he quickly schooled his features.

"I know I didn't have anything to do with that."

"So the video of you torching the police cruiser that she was standing next to is simply a coincidence?"

"Must be."

"I'm gonna be honest with you here. You're pretty much fucked. And it's not helping your cause you sitting back trying to maintain this tough guy, *I don't give a fuck* attitude. Blaze told me you were being set up. I was hoping you could shed some light as to why he thinks that."

That got Riggers' attention. He sat up straight and studied me before he answered.

"You talked to Blaze?"

"Right before I came here."

"The charges are jacked. I didn't touch that little fucker Edward. I wasn't anywhere near him. And I didn't touch Nicole Brown."

Edward was Cartwright's right-hand man, and all-around douche bag. He was also in the hospital near dead. Edward claimed Riggers had assaulted him.

"You got an alibi?"

"Yep."

Why did I feel like I was pulling teeth from a Pit bull?

"You care to share?"

"Nope."

"Christ. Do you wanna save your ass or you gonna let these dicks railroad you? You're facing attempted murder charges. The assault, destruction of property, and disorderly conduct are piddly shit. However, the

DA wants to be a dick; he can add the charge of inciting violence with a notation of a hate crime. That will add time to your sentence."

"I'm not a fucking snitch," Riggers demanded.

"Man, I didn't take you for one. I did, however, take you to be the type of man that wouldn't allow someone to take you down."

"He'll get his."

"And you'll be sitting your ass in jail when it happens."

"I'm not saying shit about shit while I'm sitting in this hellhole with eyes and ears everywhere. You think they're not listening, you're wrong. You want answers? Listen to Blaze, I got nothing to say except to ask; you stop to think why my ass is sitting in a prison cell awaiting trial instead of central booking? Did you happen to go over my file? Why was my bail hearing in a judge's chambers and bail revoked? You ask yourself those questions and see where those answers lead you. Now, we done? Today's mac and cheese day; it's the only thing that's edible in this place. And tell Blaze I'm solid."

Riggers relaxed back in his chair and looked down at his outstretched legs, cutting off any further communication.

With my palms flat on the table, I pushed myself up and leaned over the table closer to Riggers.

"I'll give your message to Blaze. Take care of yourself in here, Riggers."

He didn't acknowledge me as I exited the room, closing the door behind me. I didn't have Riggers' charging folder. I wasn't investigating the alleged assault on Graham Cartwright's assistant. But I'd be looking into it, that was for damn sure.

Graham Cartwright.

He seemed to be coming up in all my conversations today.

I waited until I was walking back to my truck and called Reid.

"How'd it go?" he asked when he picked up.

"About as well as any interview with a biker in an interrogation room while in lockup."

"That good?" Reid chuckled.

"I got problems, brother. I'm gonna need you to expand your scope from just Brown to include Graham Cartwright. There'll be a few judges to add to that list as well, but I haven't pulled Jason Riggers' sheet yet."

Reid let out a loud whistle. "The district attorney, too. Not surprised. Brown and Cartwright are thick as thieves. Apparently, in the literal sense. I'll get on that today."

"Appreciate it. I'm also going to call in Quinn Alexander. I can't go to any of the guys in the department. If Brown is dirty, who the fuck knows who else he's turned. Can you get a tap in place on both their phones?"

"Of course I can. You sure you wanna go down this path?"

"I told you, I'm ready to capsize this mother fucker. I have no issue fucking them all. And after what I learned today, I have an ace up my sleeve."

"Oh, yeah? What's that?" Reid chuckled.

"You'll have to sit back and wait, just like everybody else."

18

NORMAL

Harper

It had been almost a week since I'd gone back to work. The part-time hours were perfect. Well almost. I had plenty of time after work to fiddle around the house and relax before Mac got home from work. He was a detective, which meant his hours were unpredictable and he had been called out in the middle of the night a few times, but he had tried to be home in time for us to eat dinner together. I was finding that I was a good cook. Ava had taken me shopping again and I bought new kitchen gadgets with my own money. Mac clenched his jaw, but true to his compromise he hadn't said a word. I also went to the garden center and bought five gallons of weed and grass killer. The flower beds around the house were hopeless. It would be easier to chemically eradicate the weed forest Mac had been growing than to pull them all out by hand. That had been done. Now I was just waiting for all the ugly green stems to shrivel up and die so I could plant all the beautiful shrubs and flowers I'd bought.

I did break down and agree that Mac and I would split the cost of the new landscaping. It cost a fortune, leading to another discussion about who would be paying for what around the house. Any purchase over a thousand dollars would be discussed and split or deemed a household expense, which meant that it would fall in Mac's category. I knew he was trying to be sneaky by making this new rule, but I gave in to that as well. I figured I didn't much care so why bother arguing about it. Besides, life was too short to worry about the bullshit.

The only part that wasn't perfect about going back to work was the transportation issue. The guesthouse I'd lived in was within walking distance to Del Mar's. On the rare days it had been too cold for me to walk, there was a bus stop not even a block from my house. It dropped off literally on the corner where Del Mar's was located. Mac's house was not within walking distance and the bus ride, which I didn't mind taking but Mac flat out refused, was almost an hour. He said it was whacked for me to sit on a bus for nearly an hour due to all the stops the bus made when the actual drive time was twenty minutes tops.

Which meant he drove me to work every morning. That was a good part. I got to spend my mornings getting ready for work with Mac doing the same.

Normal.

The bad part to that was Mac had to get up two hours earlier than he normally would to drive me into work. He said he didn't mind. He enjoyed sitting at the counter eating his breakfast and catching up on the news before he had to get to the station.

However, that still wasn't the really bad part. Because Mac was across town at the precinct or out doing detective things, namely catching bad guys, he didn't have time to pick me up in the middle of the afternoon. Which meant I had to bum rides from Suzie or Ava. Both told me they didn't mind. Ava and I normally stopped to pick up lunch before she dropped me off at home and she had to rush home to get the kids off the school bus. But I felt like a mooch having to ask for a ride every day.

Today I had made a decision.

I spent some time thinking about what Suzie had said about taking my life back. Mac had pretty much said the same thing. But it hit me square in the stomach hearing Suzie talk about how quickly life can change. One moment she and Michael were making plans to take a vacation to New York. Somewhere neither had ever been and always wanted to see. And the next Suzie was near dead and they had more hospital bills than they could afford. The trip, which was the last thing on their minds, had been put off indefinitely. With all the money they owed, they'd almost lost the café, too. With some creative financing on Reid's part—which meant he was a kick-ass guy and loaned them the money personally—they were able to keep the café. Yes, Suzie understood, and she was right.

So, after much consideration and thought, I was going to talk to Mac tonight. Dinner was almost ready and Mac was on his way home. I was pacing the front room trying to get my racing thoughts in orders when I heard the garage door start to roll up on its metal track; excitement and nervousness bubbled in my belly. Mac was home.

The door to the kitchen opened, Mac walked in and scanned the pots on the stove, the huge salad bowl full of leafy greens sitting on the island, and his gaze went in search of me. His eyes hit mine, and a smile graced his lips. My legs went shaky and my heart stopped. I loved that smile. More to the point, I loved when he directed his smile toward me. It was so full of hope and promise it was almost overwhelming. That smile was mine. And if I were smart, which I was, I'd never let it go.

"How do you feel about a mini-vacation up to

Oregon? I want to learn how to whitewater raft," I blurted out.

Probably not the smoothest way to start the conversation judging by the confusion on his face.

"Okay," he said slowly. "We can probably make that happen this summer."

"Awesome."

Mac kept his eyes on me as he moved to the dining room table, draping his sport coat over the back of the chair. He still hadn't broken contact when he pulled his holster off and placed it on the table.

"Come here, baby."

I didn't make him ask twice and walked into his outstretched arms. He folded me into a hug and kissed the top of my head. He did this often, kissed my head when I fit into his embrace. I loved that Mac was so much taller than me. When he wrapped me up, I was protected, surrounded by him.

"What's going on?" he asked.

"Well. There are a few things I want to talk to you about."

His body stiffened and his arms flexed.

"Everything okay? Did something happen?"

"No," I rushed out. He still hadn't relaxed, so I went on to reassure him. "Everything is perfect."

"Dinner ready?"

"Almost."

He pulled back just enough to see my face. "Good. Let's go sit down so we can talk."

Mac broke the hug but didn't let go of my hand as he led us to the sofa. When he sat down, he pulled me down next to him, resting our entwined hands on his thigh.

"What's going on, Harper?"

I was slowly getting used to everyone calling me by my real name again. I found I liked it a whole bunch when Mac said it. Him using my real name had started to settle some of the guilt I had felt about deceiving him. I didn't have to lie anymore.

Normal.

"I think I want to go back to my natural hair color. I started bleaching it to conceal my identity. I want to start being me again."

I waited for him to laugh at me or tell me I was being silly.

He didn't. Instead, his features relaxed and his hand squeezed mine.

"I think that is a great idea."

"But it's dark brown. I'm not really a blonde."

Mac let out a bark of laughter.

"Yeah, baby, I gathered that. I've seen you in between the times you touched up your roots. If you want to go back to brown, do it. If you wanna color your hair purple, it doesn't matter to me. Whatever makes you happy."

"Really?"

"Why would you think I'd care what color your hair is?" Mac tapped my bottom lip, stopping me from biting it. "What's really going on?"

"I want to remember how to be me." I tried to explain. Mac remained quiet and allowed me to gather my thoughts. "My name is Harper Russo. I have brown hair. I'm a ballerina. I've wanted to dance since I was six. I like to read romance novels and get lost in them. I like riding bikes. I like being outdoors, out of the city and exploring nature. I like to sing bad 90's music. My favorite movie is *Good Will Hunting*. My favorite actor is Tom Selleck. My favorite color is robin's egg blue, but sometimes it's red. I like Mexican food, but my favorite is sushi." I paused for a moment, trying to remember why I had just told him all of that. "I want to be me again. You've given me the most precious gift anyone could give —my life back. I don't want to waste it. I don't want to be afraid to live. I want to be selfish and take everything."

"That's not selfish, baby. That's beautiful."

"Oh, and I want to buy a car. I've never owned one. I mean, my dad gave me one to drive when I was sixteen, but I've never purchased one on my own. I want that, too."

"So you'll have it. We'll go look at cars and you'll buy one."

"Just like that?"

"You said you wanted one, didn't you?"

"Well, yes."

"Baby, it fucking kills me that you even question something as simple as buying a car. You don't need to hide who you are to anyone. You can walk into a car dealership and buy a car. You can go into a bank and open an account. You want credit cards, get them. No more lurking in the shadows. It's time for you to start living in the sunshine again."

"The sunshine," I repeated.

"Yeah, baby. You want to go whitewater rafting, book the trip and tell me the dates. I'll get the time off work. If you want to bike ride, and dance, and read, and sing in the rain, I'm there. I am with you every step of the way. I cannot wait to watch you explore and discover more of who you are again. It is a goddamn miracle to witness."

How had I gotten so lucky to have found Mac?

"I love you," I whispered, now looking at our clasped hands. His was so much bigger than mine; I could barely see my knuckles. Another example of how Mac enveloped me, guarded me, and sheltered me from harm.

I'd never take it for granted.

"I love you, too."

"I want to change my last name. But no more fake documents. I'll change it the legal way with the courts. I want to be Harper. However, I am not a Russo."

"I'm sure we can find a way to change your last name." Mac brought our hands up to his lips, kissing my fingers. "Do you need to take dinner out of the oven? It's gonna be a while until we eat."

Oh, yay! I knew what that meant.

"I'll turn off the oven."

I jumped up and did just that, listening to Mac chuckle as I rushed to pull the enchiladas out and set them on the cooktop. I tried my hardest to act cool when I walked back into the living room but failed miserably when I saw that Mac had undone the top buttons of his dress shirt and his erection was clearly outlined under his slacks.

I started to lower my gaze when Mac stood and started to stalk toward me.

"No, baby. Not this time. I want you to look at me. Tonight, it's Aiden and Harper. Just us. No titles, no rules, no add-ons. Us. You and me learning all about what Harper wants and needs."

Holy shit, I think I just fell a little more in love with him.

"You already give me what I need and I know what I want—you."

"Well, let's see if I can do better. There's always room for a little improvement." He smiled.

"I don't know, Mac. You improve any more, I might die."

"We don't want that. I'll aim for a near-death experience."

MAC DID INDEED BRING me to the brink of death, or at least that's what I thought I was experiencing when by the fourth orgasm, I had heard angels singing and a bright beautiful light beckoning me. It turned out I'd been wrong; it wasn't death and angels singing. It was the beauty of Mac's touch, the groans of pleasure, and the flash of ecstasy that burned my eyes.

"WE'LL FIND YOU A CAR TOMORROW," Mac told me as he tucked me into his side. His voice was thick with sleep and he yawned.

"Okay."

"Night, baby."

"Night, Aiden."

Normal.

19

OFF RESERVATION

Mac

"Detective Mackenzie?" I heard called from behind me.

I slowly turned, making sure to pull my coat back enough that I had clear access to my weapon if needed. When I had fully turned in the direction of the voice, I recognized him immediately.

"I heard you've been looking for me," he said.

Callisto Suppato.

He was correct. I'd put it out on the street that I needed a word. It was a hell of a lot easier than trying to track down a mafia enforcer. Especially one that wasn't local. His father was a Capo back in New Orleans. I had done my research on his family and knew Callisto's role in the organization. Clean-up and damage control. I also knew it would take me a while to find him if he didn't want to be found.

"Mr. Suppato…"

Callisto spoke over me. "My friends call me Cal."

"Friends? Is that what we are?" I asked.

Cal chuckled. "Point made. What can I do for you?"

"I need information."

I cut right to it, no point in bullshitting and dragging this out. Cal cut his eyes at me and looked around the parking lot.

"You serious with this shit? I wasted my time coming down here to have some pi—"

"I'd be careful with your next words. I'm not real fond of criminals trying to talk shit to me. I did some digging and I know the DA had a chat with you."

"And is that against some law I'm unaware of?" He smirked.

Jesus Christ, here we go with another smartass trying to make things more difficult than they had to be.

"It is if he's trying to shake you down."

"And why would the DA want to shake me down?"

Yep, we were doing this.

"Suppato, you have to know that your reputation and that of your father's has made its way to San Fran. You're not exactly flying under the radar. I also know about your troubles and what has brought you to the sunny state of California. I give zero fucks about it. What I care about is; I have a man sitting in lockup about to go down for a bogus attempted murder charge and a woman missing. Both seem to center around two people. One of them is playing a dangerous game. I'd hate to see your woman Makenna get caught up, too."

Callisto went from relaxed to on the razor's edge of sanity at the mention of his woman's name.

"She has nothing to do with this," Cal seethed.

"Telling you like it is. I'm sure the police chief thought his daughter was untouchable, too. That's until someone snatched her right in front of him."

I needed Callisto's cooperation and I was hoping Makenna's safety was the way to get it. After a few beats, Cal seemed to have made up his mind.

"I don't know anything about Nicole Brown other than what's been making its rounds on the wire."

"That's not what I need." Cal stayed silent and glanced around. When he looked back at me, I continued, "I just need confirmation that Graham Cartwright approached and what he offered."

His eyes darkened and some of the anger returned. "Money for protection."

"Protection? Protection from whom?" I chuckled.

Who the hell did a mafia enforcer need protection from? As far as I knew, Suppato didn't have a beef with

Nico or Blaze and those two were the biggest brokers in the city. There'd be no one else who would fuck with the son of a Capo. Not even the street gangs were stupid enough to go to war with a family.

Cal didn't find my statement funny and scowled. "Protection from his office. He said he was working new deals. That his office was no longer giving out freebies, or honoring deals with Brown, and if I wanted to continue to be able to do business uninterrupted in San Francisco, he'd be taking his cut."

"What'd you tell him?" I asked.

"I told him to go fuck himself. I don't need protection from anyone."

"Bet that pissed him off."

Graham Cartwright was not turning out to be a smart man. He was trying to flex on the major players in the San Francisco underbelly. That was not going to work out well for him.

"It did. But as you said, I give zero fucks what pisses the man off. Don't think I didn't already know he hit up the Iron Claw Pres and Nico Tuscani. Both, I know, told him the same thing."

No, I hadn't known that Cartwright had approached Tuscani. Blaze was never forthright but I had suspected there had been a conversation. Something had to have pissed Cartwright off enough to go off reservation and push the charges against Jason

Riggers so hard. The DA was no longer trying to hide his cronies either. Instead, he'd left a dirty judge hanging in the wind by forcing him to have a bail hearing in chambers and have Riggers transferred out of central booking.

"Watch your back, Suppato. He's getting desperate and making mistakes."

"Anything else?" Cal asked, not acknowledging my warning.

"Nope. Thanks for your time."

With a chin lift, he was gone.

My cell vibrated in my pocket as I was walking into Reid's office. I quickly dropped the subs I was carrying on Reid's desk and pulled my phone out.

"Hey, baby," I answered.

"I'm done with work; it was a slow day. I'm gonna run by the grocery store on the way home. Anything special you want for dinner?"

I couldn't help the smile I knew I had plastered on my face. Reid rolled his eyes and reached for his sandwich.

"Nope. Whatever you make will be fine. I shouldn't be late tonight."

"Okay. I'll surprise you."

"Perfect. Drive careful. See you soon."

"Normal," she whispered.

"Normal?"

I didn't understand why her voice had gone from upbeat to barely above a whisper.

"I feel like I've waited my whole life for this. For normal. A normal conversation. A normal day. A normal life. You gave it to me."

"Baby." I felt like I'd been punched in the solar plex. All the air had been rushed from my lungs.

"Thank you for that, Aiden."

"Nothing to thank me for, Harper."

"I love that you think that. See you soon."

"Later."

I disconnected and had forgotten that I had an audience. I thought that Reid would've given me shit about the conversation he'd overheard but he didn't say a word. Instead, he looked contemplative as he unwrapped his lunch.

I followed suit and pulled my sandwich out of the paper wrapper and waited. I knew Reid had something on his mind.

"I'm happy for you," he started, and I glanced across the desk at him. "It's about damn time."

"What's that?"

"For you to be happy."

I let his words settle in my chest and soak deep. He

was right; it was time. But more than that, it was time for Harper. She'd given up two years of her life. And if she wanted *normal,* that's what she was getting. Some might say normal was boring. I'd have to disagree. Normal can be a blessing, a beautiful and peaceful existence. Harper needed some peace in her life.

"Yeah, it is," I replied, sinking my teeth into the thick crusty Italian bread, ripping a huge piece off. Marlene's Sub Shop's homemade hoagie rolls were fucking genius.

"Ava said Harper was really stoked about the new car."

I chewed my food and thought about the day we walked into the car dealership. Her eyes lit at the seemingly mundane task of looking at cars. Nothing extraordinary, yet watching Harper with childlike enthusiasm hit me straight in my chest. She had looked so carefree and happy when she spoke to the salesman. However, her face fell when she was asked about her two-year gap of credit and work history. She'd played it off like a professional. Which in a way, I guess she was. Her profession the last two years had been perfecting her con. Being able to successfully come up with a cover on a moment's notice had been what kept her alive. In the end, I had to co-sign for her. Of course, Harper argued. She wanted her independence, and I wanted it for her.

But there was nothing wrong accepting help when you need it.

"You should've seen her, man. She sat in nearly every car on the lot. I put my foot down when she started asking questions about this little Mini, electric blue with a white racing stripe. No fucking way was she driving that tin can around the city."

"Bet that didn't go over well."

It didn't, not at all. I was lucky I still had both balls intact after I told her no and left no room for discussion. I didn't care much about what she did, but I wouldn't budge when it came to her safety.

"Once she saw the new Mustangs, she forgot all about her snit. When she saw a GT with a badass chrome package in a convertible, she'd forgotten we'd even had words."

"Yeah, I can see that new convertible being an issue for me. Ava wouldn't stop talking about it after Harper took her for a drive. She's even trying to work the kid angle. Telling me how much JJ and Melly would love driving around with the top down."

Ava was a smart woman. Reid rarely told her no. If she threw in the kids, Reid didn't stand a chance; he'd give in. My guess was they'd have a new car by summer.

My phone rang again and I glanced at the caller

ID, the name on the screen reminding me why'd I come to see Reid in the first place.

Quinn Alexander.

I slid my finger across the screen to accept, put the call on speaker, and set my phone on Reid's desk.

"Quinn. Thanks for calling me back. You're on speaker. Reid's here," I told him.

"It sounded important." Quinn jumped right in.

"Are we secure?" I asked.

I really wanted a face-to-face, talking over the phone in light of everything I'd found out didn't sit well. But with Quinn's schedule and mine, it would be impossible to find time over the next few days. What I had to tell him couldn't wait.

"From my end, yes," he replied.

"I have confirmation Graham Cartwright is trying to renegotiate payoffs. The DA's hit up a few of the powerhouses in the drug trade and has begun moving down the ladder, approaching the up and comers. I'm concerned about the mid-level players. They don't have a mind for proper etiquette yet and are reckless. They believe that they can catapult themselves into the big game by a show of force. That often times leads to innocent people getting caught in the melee," I started.

"I have taps on both of their home phones and cells. Seems that the DA isn't trying to hide what he's doing moving into the PC's business. Either he doesn't care or knows that Brown is going down and won't be able to stop him from taking his payoffs. At first, I thought he just wanted a bigger cut of the action but that's not it. He's making moves to take over completely. I highly doubt that Brown's had a sudden change of heart and has decided on the straight and arrow," Reid added.

"You think the DA is planning on taking Brown out?" Quinn asked.

"That's one assumption. But I haven't heard anything on the wire about a hit being taken out. That'd be a big contract and Dustin's been monitoring all assets. There's been no chatter," Reid answered.

"What about the girl? Any closer to finding her yet?" Quinn questioned and I winced.

Reid's eyebrows shot up and a scowl crossed his face. He didn't like that I was indebted to Nico and knew that I'd have to lie to Quinn to protect myself.

"I am. I have a pretty good idea where she is." At least I could be honest about that.

"Are you gonna share?"

Quinn's inquiry hung in the room. Was I going to share? Fuck no.

"Not yet. Give me a few more days."

"What is it you need from me?" Quinn sounded like he was a tad pissed I wouldn't share the intel I had on

Nicole Brown's whereabouts, not that I knew for certain where she was or who had her. It had been conjuncture and speculation on my part. Nico never actually confirmed he had taken Nicole or for what reason.

"I can't trust my department. I don't know who Brown has on his sideline payroll—and I'm sure he has some because he'd need people on the inside to cover his tracks. I need warrants. Everything I have so far would be considered fruit from the poisonous tree. The taps we have in place aren't exactly legal; nothing will be admissible."

"And? What exactly do you have?"

"Brown's been talking about the 50K he's into Tuscani for. He's also trying to work out a deal with a gangbanger, Evan Johnson. White boy from Sacramento who goes by the street name of Loco. Grew up in the Fivers' territory and worked his way up. One of the few white kids that's made it into a position of power in a Mexican gang. His mother being half Guatemalan was his in."

"Fivers?" Quinn stopped Reid's explanation. "Word is it was a Fiver that killed Holly Springs."

"You'd be correct. They're trying to branch out into Oakland and San Francisco. They're also responsible for some of the riots. They've been showing up to the vigils for Holly and the protests demanding the police do more to stop the gangs. The Fivers stir up trouble and the peaceful protest turns violent.

"I checked Brown's bank records. He has control of an account in his ex-wife's maiden name, and, in the last month, there have been large deposits from a bank in Sacramento. After the last conversation Brown had with Johnson, there was a deposit for 50K from the same bank. That was the exact amount they'd agreed on," Reid finished.

Reid pushed a bank statement in front of me with the Sacramento deposits highlighted. I quickly did the math and added them, 250 thousand dollars. Where in the fuck was a street gang getting that kind of cash flow?

"So what's Brown's end of the deal?"

"He's allowing the Fivers to move in on Tuscani's territory," Reid told Quinn.

The marshal let out a low whistle. "That's not going to end well. Tuscani will burn the city down." Quinn observed.

He was not wrong. When Nico caught wind that the police chief had double-crossed him, he would indeed torch the city, uncaring of all the innocent people he killed along the way. It would make all the recent unrest look like a walk in the park.

"Fuck me. How fast you think you can pull a warrant?" I asked.

"Not long. You need one for Cartwright, too?"

"No. I have his balls nailed to the wall. I'm holding off taking him in until we have everything set with Brown. I don't want to tip our hand and spook the DA. We need to take them both at the same time."

"You never did tell me what evidence you had on Cartwright," Reid asked.

"Cartwright bribed Judge Barnes to railroad Jason Riggers. It was an easy trail to follow. Let's just say Barnes owed me a favor. All it took was a little nudge and he sang like a canary. He knew he was fucked and didn't want to spend his golden years in the pen. He's a smart old man and kept emails and voice mails he'd received from the DA, and he's got dirt on fifteen other judges, past and present, who are in Cartwright's pocket. He's ready to strike a deal."

I wasn't about to tell either of them what I had on Barnes. It made me sound like I was just as dirty as Brown and Cartwright. Maybe in the eyes of the law I was. Ten years ago, during a prostitution bust, Jacob and I saw Larry Barnes sneak out the maintenance entrance of the hotel where the sting had gone down. Barnes knew we saw him. If I had known then that Barnes was dirty, I would've turned him in. However, at the time, he looked like a fragile broken man who had lost his wife to cancer. It was wrong, but I looked the other way. I didn't have it in me to ruin his career after what he'd lost. Jacob felt the same way. We let him walk. I fucked up back then and the innocent men and women of the city I had sworn to protect were now paying for it. Jason Riggers was paying for it.

"I'm going to have to bring my partner, Bryan Owens, in on this—he's got the intel and contacts I don't have yet. He's going to want to know which judges are out, so he knows who's safe to approach. It might take a couple of days. I want to be certain whomever we go to isn't going to throw us to the wolves. What are you going to do with Barnes? Do I need to pick him up and put him somewhere until we can sort through the charges and round everyone up?"

"That's a good idea," I agreed. "This is a need-to-know operation—only people you trust. We have to assume Brown and Cartwright have eyes and ears everywhere."

"Agreed."

"Be safe. Call if you need me," I told Quinn.

"Later."

Quinn disconnected and before I could look up from the phone, Reid started in.

"You're fucked."

"I know that, brother."

He wasn't telling me anything I didn't already know. I *was* fucked. But I couldn't muster up any regret. I'd do it again if it meant that Harper was safe, that she could live out the rest of her life being as normal as she wanted to be.

"I have to go," I told Reid and stood up, gathering up my uneaten lunch.

"Where to?" Reid's eyes narrowed.

He knew where I had to go.

I had bought all the shit that was on my plate. It was time for me to start paying for it.

"I have a meeting," I answered.

"Yeah, you do. With the fucking devil."

20

NONNA MARIA

Harper

I loved my new car.

Loved.

Loved.

Loved it.

I got off work early today and decided before I went to the grocery store and went home I was going to drive around with the top down. It was a beautiful day, there was no sense in wasting it. I had nowhere in particular to go, just cruising the streets, the wind blowing in my hair, radio on, high on life.

I couldn't remember a time I had ever been this happy. Mac was... perfect. The perfect combination of protective, in control, demanding and gentle, sweet, loving. He had no problem being demonstrative and showing me how much he loved me. He was always touching me, cuddling me, and holding me close. Why had I fought him for so long? Frankie Russo, that's why. It was easy to forget now that Mac had shown me what it meant to live again. I hadn't given my brother a second thought. Mac had me wrapped up in a bubble. I liked it there. I didn't have to worry about much of anything. I was... happy.

That's what I was thinking when I pulled up to a red light and stopped. The smell of garlic and tomatoes had me craving a good lasagna. One like my Nona used to make with layers of melty cheese and crumbled sausage and veal. I could eat a whole tray of Nona's famous dish. I glanced around at the restaurants and shops, with the top down all the sights and smells of Little Italy were unobstructed. On the corner, there was a bistro ironically named Nonna Maria's, that was my grandmother's name. I giggled at the coincidence and when I turned back to the traffic in front of me, something caught my attention.

Mac was walking out of the restaurant. Even from a distance I could tell he looked pissed. His hands were on his hips, his face to the heavens. The door behind him opened and Mac turned to see who had followed him out. A good-looking man in a suit with dark hair and olive complexion stuck his hand out in Mac's direction, handing him something. Mac took it and put it in his pocket.

The more I stared at the man with Mac it became clear who Mac was talking to. Nico Tuscani. Even if my brother wasn't Frankie Russo Mob Boss, I still would've recognized Nico Tuscani. Pretty much everyone knew of Nico. He'd been in the news enough on charges of racketeering. Yet, he always got off, nothing ever stuck. Witnesses vanished or evidence went missing.

What the hell was Mac doing shaking a mob boss's hand in front of a restaurant?

Mac nodded and started to walk down the street and just like that, the bubble burst.

When the light turned green, I slowly pulled forward, thankful for the afternoon traffic. I didn't want Mac to see me. My mind was racing and all thoughts of normalcy flew out the window as I went back into self-preservation mode. Had Mac set me up? Had he known who I was all along? Had he made a deal with Nico to turn me over to Frankie?

I had to hurry and pack. I had to be gone before Mac got home. But there was one thing I had to do first. This time I was not going to sneak away like a coward.

Once the traffic broke I sped, trying to reach my destination. I pulled into Ava's driveway and cut the engine. I hightailed it to the front door and impatiently waited for her to answer.

"Hey. I wasn't expecting you." She smiled and opened the door for me to enter.

No, I guess she wasn't. I also wasn't expecting the man I loved to have lied to me.

"Sorry to drop in but I needed to come over to say goodbye."

"Goodbye?" Her brow scrunched up and she tilted her head. "Are you and Mac going somewhere?"

Of course, she would think that.

"No. Um, just me. I don't have time to explain. But I didn't want to leave like I did last time without telling you how much your support and friendship has meant to me. You've been the best friend I've ever had."

And I meant that. I'd never been close to anyone, even before I had to run.

"What do you mean leave? What's going on?"

"I'm sorry. I really don't have time to talk right now. I have to go. I'll try to contact you soon."

I reached to give her a hug, but she stepped back. "Harper! What's going on? You're scaring me."

"What's scaring you, Ava baby?" Reid's voice boomed from behind me.

How had I missed him coming in the house? Ava always complained how silent he was when he entered a room, but I'd never experienced it.

Ava looked over my shoulder, then back to me. I

hoped she could read my expression. I was silently begging her not to say anything.

I knew I was fucked when her hands slid into mine and she squeezed. "I'm your friend. I'm not letting you leave here until you tell us what's wrong. You are not doing this alone again."

"I'm fine. Promise," I lied.

"Bullshit. You came here to say goodbye." Ava's voice had become two octaves higher than normal. "We can help you if you're in danger. But I swear to God, Harper, you're not running again. Where's Mac? Is he okay?"

I shouldn't've come here. I'd forgotten how protective my friend was. She was fierce when she thought someone she loved was upset or hurt.

"Shit," I whispered. I was screwed. Why was Reid here anyway? "Mac's fine. I really need to get going. Besides, I don't want to intrude on family time. I'll call you later."

I pulled my hands free and turned just in time to see Mac fill the open front door. He stopped just inside the house, did a full body scan from top to toe, and scowled. "What's wrong, Harper? Are you hurt? Did something happen?"

I took a step back and bumped into Ava. Mac cut his eyes, looking from me to Reid and he tried again. "What happened?"

"I got here and Harper was saying she was scared but wanted to say goodbye to Ava," Reid told Mac.

I glared at Reid, wishing I could shoot lasers out of my eyes. I was up shit's creek. There was no way Mac was going to let me leave without an explanation.

"Don't look at me like that, Harper." Reid smirked.

Ass!

"You called him," I accused.

"Damn right, I did. I'd shoot his ass if something was upsetting Ava and he didn't tell me."

"What's going on?" Ava asked.

"Harper thinks she saw something and she is getting ready to overreact. I'm trying to stop that from happening," Reid answered his wife.

"Overreact?" I practically yelled, thankful that Melly and JJ were at school.

"Yes, Harper. Why don't you ask Mac what he was doing with Nico?"

Well, fuck me running. How did Reid know what I saw unless he was in on Mac's plan?

Mac stepped into the house and shut the door behind him. I was trapped. There was no way I could get through both men and out the front door. I could try to go out the back and run but I wouldn't get very far.

They wouldn't hurt me in front of Ava or in Reid's family home, right?

"Ask me," Mac demanded.

I shook my head. I didn't want to hear the words. My heart was already shattered. Hearing Mac tell me he was involved in the mob would only further devastate me.

I should've known better than to hope. Happiness was never in the stars for me.

21

WE'RE OVER

Mac

What. The. Fuck?

Harper was standing across the living room, shaking like a leaf and looking at me as if the sight of my very existence disgusted her. Reid obviously knew more than he was saying. When he called me and told me to get to his house ASAP, I didn't ask why when I heard the urgency in his tone. My gut twisted when I pulled up and saw Harper's new car in his driveway. My first thought was she'd been hurt but when I walked in and saw her standing in the living room, I was somewhat relieved.

"What's wrong, Harper? Are you hurt? Did something happen?" I asked.

She didn't answer me; instead, she backed away from me, bumping into Ava.

"What happened?" I asked Reid.

"I got here and Harper was saying she was scared but wanted to say goodbye to Ava," Reid told me.

Harper threw Reid a dirty look and tried to move around Ava. Instead of allowing Harper to retreat, Ava put a protective arm around Harper.

"Don't look at me like that, Harper," Reid said.

What the hell was going on? Why was Harper saying goodbye to Ava?

"You called him." Harper scowled.

"Damn right, I did. I'd shoot his ass if something was upsetting Ava and he didn't tell me."

"What's going on?" Ava asked.

"Harper thinks she saw something and she is getting ready to overreact. I'm trying to stop that from happening." Reid crossed his arms over his chest and settled in.

"Overreact?" Harper yelled.

"Yes, Harper. Why don't you ask Mac what he was doing with Nico?"

My whole world tilted.

Fuck. She saw me with Nico. I didn't know how Reid knew, and I didn't care at the moment.

"Ask me," I demanded.

Harper didn't answer, instead she pulled away from Ava and glanced around the room like a cornered wild animal.

"Do you really think that I would hurt you?" I asked in utter disbelief.

Now that I knew she wasn't hurt or in danger, I was beginning to get pissed. How the hell could the woman I love think I would harm her? She still wasn't talking but she continued to inch her way toward the kitchen, placing more distance between us.

After everything I had done for this woman, she was backing away from me like I was the enemy. In three strides, I was in the middle of the living room only feet from her. Her eyes widened in fear and her face paled.

"You do not back away from me like I'm some monster that's going to hurt you. If you're pissed, you stay and fight. Yell, scream, I don't care. What you don't do is run—like a coward. And have the decency to tell me what you think I've done."

"I saw you with Nico Tuscani," she blurted.

"So?"

"He's a mob boss."

"Believe me, Harper, I am well aware of what he is."

"What, is he working with my brother to off me so he can collect on the hit?" she asked, making my temper rise.

"Seriously?"

Reid was shaking his head and Ava's eyes were

darting around trying to piece together what was going on. Shit, that made two of us. I was unclear how Harper had made that assumption by seeing me with Nico but it was jacked.

"Yes, seriously. My brother has been trying to kill me for years. Are you in on it, too? Is that why you're meeting with Nico, huh? Are you gonna turn me over to them now?"

"Jesus Christ," Reid muttered.

Ava sucked in a breath and covered her mouth.

"Completely jacked. Harper, why don't you think about what you're saying? Really think about what you know about me, and fuck, about Reid for that matter. Do you really think I'd let anyone put their hands on the woman I love? And before you answer, really think about it."

She didn't answer. Instead, she asked, "Why were you meeting with Nico?"

I thought about lying and telling her it was police business and I couldn't tell her, which was partially the truth, but mostly not.

"You sure you want the answer to that question?" I asked.

"Yes." Came immediately. I looked at Reid, asking if he wanted to have Ava leave the room before I told Harper why I was with Nico.

"Ava baby, come here."

I waited for her to walk to Reid. He pulled her close and tucked her to his side.

"I was meeting with Nico Tuscani this afternoon because I needed information from him about a case." Her shoulders slumped forward and relief washed over her face. I could've left it at that, the half-truth, but I couldn't. If there was any chance that Harper and I were going to go the distance, I wasn't going to start lying to her. "And because I owe him a marker. He's called it in and now I owe him information as well."

"Why do you owe a mobster a favor?" The panic and accusation was back in her voice.

"Because I asked him to kill someone for me."

I watched Harper closely—her eyes widened, her face twisted, and her hands balled up in fists.

"You what? Who?" Harper yelled.

"Your brother. I called in a favor at the prison. The guard turned his back while a few of Nico's guys went into Frankie's cell and took care of him. In exchange for the hit, I owe Nico a marker. Nico is in the process of dismantling the Russo family assets and claiming the territory that your family once controlled. Nico is also offering you his protection. He's put the word out that you are not to be touched—by anyone."

"Why would you do that?" Harper cried.

"Normal," I answered.

"What?"

"The other day you thanked me for giving you normal. A normal life, a normal conversation, a normal day. That's why I did it. So you could be free to have normal."

"I can't believe you did that. You know how much I hate the mob. I told you what being involved with them has done to me. Now you're in bed with a mob boss and calling in hits yourself."

What was left of my temper was gone.

"You're goddamn right I called in a hit on your brother. The man has been terrorizing you for years. He hired someone to kill you!" I damn near yelled. "Now I owe on that. I knew full well what I was doing when I made the deal. I know Nico Tuscani now owns me. I might never get out from under him. But you're alive and untouchable. You'll able to walk the streets, live your life, and not have to be afraid. I would change nothing. I would choose your life over mine every day. Now, here's where you decide if you can live with what I've done."

"You have no idea what you've done." Harper stepped back and shook her head. "I can't be here anymore. You shouldn't have made that deal, Mac. You'll never be free. I can't do this. I can't!"

"Can't do what, Harper?" I asked.

"I love you, Mac. But we're over. I can't be with you."

Harper turned her back to me and I heard Ava's sobs mingling with Harper's. I looked at Reid, hugging a crying Ava close, and my heart ached to grab Harper and comfort her, beg her not to leave me, not to give up on us.

But, I didn't. Without a word, I headed for the door. Call it anger or pride but I couldn't fight for us if she was willing to throw us away. I'd been wrong. I thought my love for her could get us through anything.

So fucking wrong.

22

I WANT BABIES

Harper

The door slammed.

Reid cursed.

Ava cried.

What just happened? How did I let Mac walk out the door? Why didn't I stop him, talk to him, beg him to run away with me so we could be safe?

He didn't understand what he'd done. Making a deal with Nico meant he'd forever be in the mob's debt. I'd never be safe, neither would he. Nico would take and take and the minute Mac said no, Nico would turn on him and both our lives would be in danger. Reid and Ava's, too. Anyone who was close to Mac would be used against him.

Oh, God! Melly and JJ!

"Reid. You have to help him. Please," I begged.

"Help him with what?" he bit out.

I didn't blame Reid for being angry with me; he loved Mac, they were like brothers.

"I know you hate me, but Mac is in danger. Nico will never leave him alone. You have to make Mac understand."

"You don't think Mac understands exactly what he's done?" he growled. "That man loves you so much he's compromised his own moral code to make sure you'd be safe—in a real way. Your family can never come after you now. And that's because Mac made that happen."

"My family can't, but Nico can. That's the way the mob works. Nico will come after us all as soon as Mac stops giving Nico what he wants."

Reid's body locked and Ava inhaled. Thank God, he was getting it now.

"I'm going to explain one thing and it's more for my wife's peace of mind than yours. Nico Tuscani is not an issue for any of us. There's not a snowball's chance in hell I'd let Mac get near him if I didn't know I had the situation under control. Mac and Nico have a one-time deal. Nico has called in his debt. It's something that Mac can handle. No one is going to get hurt, no one's dying, Mac's exposure is very minimal. As far as dealing with the mob is concerned, it's tame." Reid was delusional, too. I grew up with men like Nico, I knew the way this worked. "I see you don't believe me. And right now, I'm so mad at you I don't fucking care. But I know Mac would care and he wouldn't want you scared. And I know my wife cares about you. Nico has asked Mac to look the other way on an investigation. Mac is willing to do that. One, because he owes Nico, but mostly because it has to do with a dirty cop. So Mac is looking the other way while the situation plays out. Lastly, I'll explain why Nico will never come after you, Mac, or my family when this is done. Nico and I have an understanding. In my line of work, I have a whole lot of dirt on a whole lot of people. The dirt I have is the kind that no one wants seeing the light of day. It's in everyone's best interest for it to stay buried."

"You're blackmailing him?" I asked. Was everyone crazy? My brother would slit someone's throat if they tried that.

"Call it whatever you want. Nico and I have a mutual agreement and understanding. That's all you need to know."

My head was a little dizzy and my stomach was twisted into knots. I wasn't sure if I was going to throw up or if I was going to pass out. I was grateful when Ava made her way to me and tugged me to the couch.

"Sit," she suggested and I slumped down into the overstuffed cushions, wishing they could swallow me up and I could sink into oblivion, far away from the fucked-up situation I now found myself in. My life had gone to shit again, in one afternoon. I was transported back in a bad case of déjà vu. The only thing that was missing was the beating my brother had delivered.

My brother.

Frankie was dead and I didn't know how I felt about that. Did it make me just as much of a monster as him that I was relieved, happy even, that he was gone? I tried to think of us as children, a time when we used to play together and laugh and tease each other, but I failed. The last two years had wiped my memory clean of any good thoughts of the brother I'd once loved. He'd erased all gratitude and adoration I once had for him. He'd turned into a stone-cold killer. A mobster.

Reid handed me a bottle of water and sat on the coffee table in front of me.

"I want you to listen to me carefully, Harper, before it's too late. Mac is the best man I know. There is no one I would trust more with my family than him. You may be scared, shocked, and even pissed at Mac. But you have to know, he did what he did because he loves you. You didn't see the hurt you caused when he thought Quinn was your man. You didn't see him out of his mind with worry when you ran and he learned the truth about who you are. And if you didn't see the devastation on his face just now, then you're blind.

That man loves you. What you need to do now is dig deep and sort your shit out."

"Sort my shit out?" I huffed. "You have no idea what men like Nico are capable of."

"Don't I? You know what I do for a living. I see firsthand what organized crime does to the city. Every day I go to work and have to deal with the most disgusting men and women humanity offers. I know what Frankie did to you. I've seen the pictures and read the reports. So did Mac. He read through your file front to back, pulled up every article he could find on Frankie Russo and memorized each of his crimes. He didn't make the decision to have your brother killed lightly. He did it because Frankie Russo was an animal that had to be put down."

"He saw the pictures?" I asked.

How humiliating. Frankie had damn near killed me. It took me a month before I'd look at myself in a mirror and when I did, I was horrified at the reflection staring back at me. I couldn't imagine what the pictures looked like that Mac had seen. Why would he want to see those?

"He did. Frankie is gone and you're free. You can live your life being anyone you want, anywhere you want. Don't throw that in Mac's face and turn on him."

"But he knows I loathe anything that has to do with

the mob," I said. My protest sounded weak, even to my own ears.

Shit. What had I done?

"He didn't join the mob, Harper."

I took a moment to mull over what Reid had said and compare it to what I knew about Mac. I was still pissed he'd made a deal with a mobster and hadn't told me. But wasn't that my fault? When he said we were safe to leave the house, he'd told me outright he wouldn't lie to me, he'd tell me what had happened. I was the one that had decided to live with my head in the clouds. I knew deep down in my bones that Mac would never harm me, yet I accused him of setting me up. I had no excuse for behaving the way I had toward him. Even if the shock of seeing him with Nico scared the hell out of me—still did—I knew better.

Damn.

"Did I overreact?" I asked Ava. She was level-headed and honest. I trusted her to tell me the truth.

"Yes. But I understand why. I get that you're scared and seeing Mac with Nico was a shock. But, Harper, once he explained, you should've talked it out with him."

"Shit."

Forgetting everything I knew about how protective Mac was over his friends, especially the kids, Reid would have Mac's back. He'd never let anything harm them or Mac. I'd been on my own for so long I reacted poorly. I didn't think.

But why didn't Mac stay? He told me not to run like a coward, yet that's what he did.

"Mac left," I noted lamely.

"Yeah, honey, he did. You told him it was over and turned your back to him," Ava whispered.

"Why? Why didn't he force me to understand?" I cried.

"Honestly? Because he's been fighting for you for damn near a year. He's pushed you to open up to him and you refused. He's chased you and you've denied him. But the real reason he left, he doesn't think he's good enough for you." Reid's words were like a cold hard slap in the face. He was right. I had done all those things.

I pushed him away even though I was in love with him. I refused to let him in even though I wanted nothing more than for Mac to wrap me up in his arms. But I did all that because I loved him; I was trying to protect him.

"I didn't want him to get hurt. I couldn't let him in. I wanted to protect him. Why would he think he's not good enough? That's crazy."

"Because he thinks he's done questionable things and that makes him a bad guy. He admitted to having your brother whacked and you basically compared him to a mob boss."

"Shit. I know he's not. I'm just scared. How do I fix this? I have to go and talk to him."

I tried to stand but Ava put her hand on my leg and stopped me.

"Not right now you don't. Give him a few hours to calm down. I know Mac has a bad temper. If you go to him now, while he's hurt, he'll say a bunch of stuff he doesn't mean," she warned.

"Then I'll take it. I deserve to hear it after what I did."

"That's not a good idea," Reid added.

"Would you let Ava stew for a few hours if she was pissed, even if you knew you'd get the hot side of her tongue?"

"No, I wouldn't." Reid smirked. "You got your shit sorted? Because he's gonna push you away and maybe say some jacked shit to you. Either you sit tight and let him calm down or you gotta roll with it. Be strong enough to put him in his place and call him on his shit. He's hurt and the fact that he loves you and had envisioned a life with a white picket fence and babies has compounded it a hundred-fold."

"He thought about babies?" I asked.

"What the fuck do you think Mac's been doing with you? He made a deal with the devil to make sure you were safe. Do you think he'd do that if he wasn't planning a forever with you?"

"I didn't think," I admitted. "I want babies with him. I want the house and the kids and I want to crawl into bed with him every night exhausted because I've been chasing our kids all day," I blurted out, uncaring that I sounded like a totally crazy person. Going from hysteria to declarations of love. "Thank you both. I'm solid, promise. I need to go find Mac."

"Good luck." Ava smiled.

"Don't take shit from him," Reid reminded me. "He's gonna try and walk away. Don't let him. He's gonna try and shock you, too, telling you the worst things he's ever done. Mac is my brother. I only want what is best for him, and if I didn't think you were strong enough for him, I wouldn't let you go. Be tough and remember that he loves you."

"Okay."

I patted my pocket, confirming my keys and cell phone were there and headed for the door.

"What do I do if he leaves the house?" I asked, knowing that if Mac didn't want to stay, there was nothing I could physically do to stop him.

"Then you call me," Ava said. Reid was staring at his wife with a smile so wide it took my breath away. Ava might've looked like a petite shy woman but she was a force to be reckoned with. Ava was no pushover and she'd have no issues going toe-to-toe with Mac if needed.

I rushed to my car and hoped like hell Mac had gone home. It didn't take long to pull into his neighborhood and I was both grateful and scared shitless when I saw his car was in the driveway. I'd spent the time on the drive over fortifying my resolve, but now that I was faced with the confrontation I was scared again. What if I screwed this up? What if he didn't forgive me and kicked me out?

I wouldn't let him. I couldn't. I loved him too much to accept his denial.

Mac loved me.

He wanted babies with me.

I kept repeating those two things on the walk from my car to the front door.

Did I knock? Use my key? Should I sit in my car and give him a few hours to calm down?

Was I being totally screwy and emotionally unbalanced?

I totally was.

Fuck it. Time to fix this and remind my man that we were in this together—for the long haul.

I opened the door and my breath caught in my throat.

23

LET HER GO

Mac

I looked down at the shattered glass on the floor, then at the dent in my drywall and not for the first time wondered why I was such a dumbass. I was a grown man, a detective, a Dom. Losing my temper and causing damage to my own belongings... weak.

I heard the gasp from the front door right about the same time the tumbler of whiskey hit the wall. What I didn't hear was Harper shutting the front door and strutting her ass into the house, coming to a stop in front of the mess on the floor. She looked at me with sad eyes and I got pissed all over again. I'd waited months to see those eyes unguarded and full of love. I'd fought and been patient knowing the payoff would be pure beauty. And it was. For a little over a week, Harper had been in my bed and in my space. I had the pleasure of looking into those eyes every morning I'd woken up, and every night before I'd fallen asleep with her in my arms.

For a goddamned week, my life had been perfect. Now it was gone. I actually didn't blame her. Frankie was gone, she was safe, and now she could move on with a respectable man that could give her the life she deserved. Not some hotheaded cop with blood on his hands.

She knelt down and started picking up the larger shards of glass.

"Stop, Harper, you'll cut yourself. Why are you here?"

"We need to talk," she said, completely dismissing my command as she continued to pick up the broken pieces.

"Think you said it all, babe."

"I didn't say the important stuff, the stuff I meant to say." She stood and walked past me to the kitchen. She tossed the glass in the trash and turned to face me. I braced for the onslaught of criticism but when she spoke again, I was shocked. "I forgot to tell you thank you for helping me at the truck stop. Thank you for protecting me. Thank you for making the deal with Nico to save my life. I should've trusted you. I know you would never hurt me and I said some shitty things I hope you can forgive me for. Thank you for loving me enough to put your life in danger to save mine. But most of all, thank you for not giving up on me when I was pushing you away."

Was this a trick? I felt like I was in the Twilight Zone or maybe the little midget was going to walk in the front door and escort me to the plane to Fantasy Island. When I left Reid's, Harper had made it clear we were done.

"I think you meant what you said when we were at Reid's. I did make a deal with the mob and just because you're standing here now saying flowery shit doesn't change that. I'm not going to renege on my agreement because you find it distasteful."

"I know. I'm sorry."

"What happens the next time you find out I've done something you don't like? You gonna turn your back on me then, too?"

"No, that was wrong."

I wasn't sure what game she was now playing but I needed to leave before I said something ridiculous like I love you and I cannot live without you.

"I got shit to do. I'll leave so you can pack or do whatever it is you came here to do."

"No, Aiden, please. I came here to talk this out. I'm not packing. I'm not going anywhere."

"There's nothing to talk about, Harper. You proved today you'll cut and run when shit goes bad."

I was being an ass and I knew it, but it was better this way. Better she left now before we got in any deeper. Who the fuck was I kidding? I was already in deep. She was so encased in my heart there'd never be any hope of evicting her. I was pissed about that, too. The promise of her had proved to be so great that I was forever ruined. No other woman could compare. She was it for me and she'd turned her back on us.

"That's not fair. I was shocked and scared. You know my history. I admit I reacted poorly, worse than that actually. But it took me less than thirty minutes to realize my mistake and come after you. I'm sorry."

She was right; it had taken her less than an hour to come over, but I couldn't risk it.

"It did. But it's too late. There will be other things you'll find out. Things that are worse than putting out a hit on your piece of shit brother and when you find out about them, you'll run."

"Try me, Aiden."

I had to hand it to her. She stood her ground with her little arms crossed over her chest, looking like she was ready to go toe-to-toe with me.

"Not a chance. I don't trust you."

"It's not that you don't trust me; it's because you're scared."

"What the hell does that mean?"

"This has nothing to do with what I said. You're

pushing me away because you're scared. Today was a reminder of how much you love me. How much it would kill you if we didn't work out. Today I hurt you and now you're scared and you're going to punish both of us. I can handle anything you throw my way, Mac. I'm not leaving."

"Is that so?"

"Yep."

She stayed perfectly still and smirked at me.

"You know, it's cute when you act all tough and strong. You want to know how I know you'll run a mile when I tell you the things I've done?" I didn't wait for her to answer before I continued. "Because the things I've done disgust *me*. I killed the man who murdered Jacob." Harper's face was devoid of any emotion. "I didn't kill him in the line of duty, Harper. Remember months ago when I texted you out of the blue and told you to get home, that I needed you? I came to you to fuck my guilt away. I used you. I'd just finished putting a bullet in Jimmy Kelley, Jacob's brother, and came to you with blood on my hands. I'm a murderer."

Harper now had tears streaming down her cheeks. I was finally getting through to her.

"I don't believe you," she whispered.

"You should. I shot him in the forehead execution style."

"No, I mean, I don't believe that you murdered him."

"Well, then what the fuck would you call taking someone's life?"

"Protection. Love. Loyalty. Defense. All the same reasons you had Frankie taken out."

"You make me sound better than I am. I killed Jimmy out of revenge. He killed my best friend. My partner, Ava's husband, JJ's father. I killed him because he destroyed a family and I fucking hated him."

"No, you didn't. You killed Jimmy because he was a threat to Ava and JJ. I remember what happened. Jimmy showed up drunk at Ava's. She was nice enough to let her brother-in-law spend the night. The next morning someone had shot up her front yard, Jimmy had pulled a gun on JJ, he'd had money and drugs on him. Reid lost his mind, too. Jimmy was dangerous and a gangbanger that had killed his own brother. He had no problem hurting Ava and JJ. You killed him to protect them."

"Whatever you need to think to make yourself feel better. But I know the truth. I know what type of man I am. I'm not good for you. I'm not your happily ever after."

It was time to face the truth about myself. I hadn't been able to protect Jacob and he was gunned down in an alley alone. I didn't protect Ava and she'd been stalked and kidnapped. Hell, I hadn't even been good enough for my money-grubbing ex-wife; she needed to fuck her yoga instructor to get all the things she was missing from our marriage. I'd been a shit husband, putting my job first. After she'd left, I used every woman in the greater San Francisco area to fuck away my shortcomings. I was an asshole. Harper deserved better.

My phone vibrated and I pulled it out. Checking the caller ID, I was relieved Quinn was finally getting back to me.

"Mac," I greeted.

"We have a meeting with Judge Fox at his home in Presidio Heights. Can you be there in thirty?" Quinn asked, not wasting any time.

"Absolutely. I'll call Reid. Text me the address."

"Bring everything you have, even the wiretaps. Judge Fox will want to hear them."

"You think that's wise? Reid's guys didn't exactly follow procedure," I reminded him.

"Positive. My partner Owens is a personal friend of Judge Fox. He's already filled him in."

I wasn't entirely comfortable with Quinn and his partner telling a judge Reid had illegal wire taps on the district attorney and the police chief but I had to trust Quinn knew what he was doing. If Quinn trusted Owens, and Owens trusted Judge Fox, I had no choice but to roll with it. Quinn was my only hope of getting the warrants.

"Copy that. We'll see you in thirty."

Quinn didn't offer a goodbye and disconnected. Before I could pocket my phone, a text from an unknown number came through with an address. I needed to call Reid and get going. Presidio Heights was a thirty-minute drive with no traffic and I still had to deal with Harper.

"I have to go," I told Harper, sharper than I should've.

"Please stay. We have to talk."

"I can't, Harper, I have to work. There's a break in my case."

I waited for her to bring up Nico and ask if I was going to meet with him, but it never came.

"Be safe. I'll be here when you get back."

"You shouldn't be. Pack your stuff, move on, and find a nice man to settle down with. You'll be better off. Trust me, I can't be what you need."

I grabbed my holster and secured it on my belt before I swung my leather jacket over my arm and headed for the door.

"You already are what I need. I don't want you to *give* me happily ever after, Aiden. I'm willing to fight for it. I'll claw, bite, and bleed for it as long as it's with you. We can have it all; the babies, the white picket fence, a beautiful life. All I need is for you to fight with me."

Her words almost made me stop. I wanted nothing more than to pull her into my arms and take what she offered. But I couldn't. I was right; she deserved better. After everything that her brother had put her through, she'd earned herself a nice safe life. I couldn't give her that.

I love you, Harper. The sentence never left my mouth as I closed the door behind me.

After firing off a quick text to Reid about our meeting with Judge Fox, I was on the road to the address Quinn had sent me. The thirty-minute drive felt like five as I replayed Harper's heartfelt plea over and over in my mind. Was I being completely unreasonable? By the time I pulled in front of the house and saw Quinn standing outside, I had begun to doubt myself. What if we could make it work? The agony on her face when I left was flipping around in my gut, making it hard to concentrate on the meeting that was about to take place.

I had to stop thinking about Harper. I made the right decision. It didn't matter how much I loved her, I had to let her go.

24

SHE WAS DETERMINED

Mac

"Thanks for coming on such short notice," Quinn greeted when I met him on the sidewalk.

"I'm the one who should be thanking you. Before we go in, what can you tell me about Fox?" I asked, looking over Quinn's shoulder at what was more than likely a twenty-million-dollar home.

"I know what you're thinking. Judge Fox comes from money as did his late wife. Owens says Fox can be trusted, but I still looked into him. Called a black-ops friend in Tampa who works with one of the best hackers around. The guy could probably tell you every digital footprint Fox has ever left, plus what time he takes a shit every day. Everything Owens told me checked out—the judge is clean."

I didn't know if it was simply good instincts that

made Quinn a good marshal, or if it was hard-earned from years on the job. Either way, I felt better knowing that he'd looked into the judge's background.

Reid pulled up and both of us watched as he got out of his Rover and made his way over to us.

"Quinn, this is Logan Reid." I made the introductions remembering they'd never met in person.

"Pleasure," Reid said and offered Quinn his hand.

"Nice to meet you," Quinn greeted.

"What can you tell us about Fox?" Reid asked.

Quinn chuckled before he answered. "Damn, you two think alike. I was explaining to Mac before you got here—Fox checked out. The money's from family. I had a black-ops friend, whom I trust implicitly, discreetly dig through the judge's financials. He's squeaky clean. As far as we can tell, he doesn't even take all the tax deductions he should. Either his accountant sucks or he doesn't mind paying the extra money to the government. Owens—my partner—his mother was good friends with the judge's mother, and both were members of the American Legion Ladies Auxiliary. Mrs. Fox has passed away but the families are still in touch."

"How are we gonna play this?" Reid asked, but before I could answer another car pulled up. Both Quinn and Reid turned to scrutinize the driver.

"Is that Larry Barnes?" Reid inquired, pulling his sunglasses off to get a better look.

"Sure is," I told him.

"Your ace." He laughed.

"Yep."

"Care to fill me in?" Quinn turned to me, obviously not pleased with my surprise.

"Judge Barnes is here to guarantee our warrants," I told him.

"Larry," I greeted when he joined our huddle.

"Afternoon, Detective." Larry was less than pleased to be here. However, he had no choice. His only hope now was to beg Judge Fox for leniency.

"Why don't we take this inside," Quinn suggested and turned toward the long walk up to the house. "Owens is with the judge."

Without bothering to knock, Quinn let himself in the house, the rest of us following down a long corridor. So this was how the other half lived? The inside was even more impressive than the exterior. Mahogany wainscoting paneling gave a rich warm feel to a hall which opened into a library that was equally impressive. An older man sat behind an ornate desk, assessing us as we entered the room. Both him and another man, I assumed was Owens, stood to greet us.

Once the formalities were complete, Judge Fox sat

back down and without any unnecessary pleasantries began.

"Deputies Alexander and Owens gave me a preliminary outline. However, before I can issue an arrest warrant for the district attorney of San Francisco, I need more than assumption and conjecture." The judge raised a bushy eyebrow and looked between me and Reid. "You do understand the implications of your accusations if you're wrong? It won't just be you, Detective, on the receiving end of a reprimand. I, too, will be held accountable. While my interest is certainly piqued, and I've heard rumors over the years, I will not risk my career or Graham Cartwright's, based on rumor. Please tell me you have solid evidence to back up your accusations."

"I do, your Honor. Judge Barnes?" I turned to Larry, motioning him to come forward. The man seemed to have aged twenty years in the last week. I felt bad for the man. A onetime moment of weakness after his wife had passed away had ruined him.

"You have to know I am deeply ashamed of my actions," Judge Barnes began. "Ten years ago, I paid for sexual favors from a woman that was provided by an escort service. Shortly thereafter, I was approached by Graham Cartwright." Barnes took a moment to gather his thoughts. The agony that crossed his face was painful to witness. "He had photographs of me in compromising positions with the prostitute. Cartwright began blackmailing me. In the beginning, it was small things like dismissing evidence a defense attorney presented. As the years went on, his demands increased." Barnes stopped and held Judge Fox's stare.

"And what are his current demands?" Judge Fox bit out.

"His latest request was to charge Jason Riggers with aggravated assault and attempted murder."

"And?" Fox questioned.

"Graham had no evidence to substantiate his allegations. He requested a bond hearing in my chambers, which I heard and denied ROR and bond. Riggers is currently being held at California State Prison."

"Where was Mr. Riggers' attorney?" the judge asked.

"Cartwright failed to notify the defendant's counsel," Barnes answered.

"So, the case will be thrown out. Right?" Fox questioned.

The room was silent for a moment. This was the part of the story that told the level of corruption that was running rampant in the DA's office.

"Not if it is brought before me. Cartwright demanded I allow the case to be heard and do everything I can to make sure Riggers is found guilty of attempted murder. Then I'm supposed to give the maximum sentence allowed."

"Jesus Christ, Larry." Fox ran a hand down his face in disbelief before pointing an angry finger at his colleague. "I want exact clarification; San Francisco's District Attorney, Graham Cartwright, told you outright, and in no uncertain terms, to fix the trial so the jury has no choice but to find Jason Riggers guilty of attempted murder in the first degree, even if the evidence didn't support the charge?"

"Yes. And Riggers is only the latest."

The anger rolling off Judge Fox was palpable. His face was a shade darker than fire engine red and his hands were clenched into fists on his desk. I looked to both marshals standing off to the side and they mirrored the judge's irritation.

"How many others?" Fox asked.

"Countless." Barnes cleared his throat again and continued, "I asked my clerk to bring ten boxes filled with case files to my home. Each box contains a year's worth of cases that Cartwright prosecuted in my court-room. You'll have to subpoena the actual transcripts, but this will give you a head start. I'll save you the trouble of a search warrant and give you permission to enter and search my home. You'll find everything you need in my private office. I've already given Mr. Reid consent to wiretap my home, cell, and office phones and I've turned over voice recordings of conversations between Cartwright and myself, dating back to almost the beginning. Once I realized how bad it was going to get, I started recording everything. I knew it was only a matter of time. I know there's no excuse, but, at first, I was terrified my children would find out about the prostitute. It would have killed them after losing their mother. By the time I came to my senses, I was in too deep with Cartwright. I should have come clean a long time ago."

"But you stuck your fucking head in the sand and hoped it would just go away, but it didn't," Owens said distastefully.

Barnes bit his lip and nodded. "And I'm not the only one. I know of fourteen other judges, past and present, Cartwright has had in his pocket."

He pulled a folded piece of paper from the jacket of his sport coat and placed it on the desk. Wide-eyed, Fox picked it up and scanned a list of names. "Son of a bitch. There's proof?"

"I have enough to get you started on search warrants."

No one spoke while Judge Fox processed the information that now-disgraced Judge Barnes had presented. Fox broke the silence, and when he did, there was no mistaking his intent.

"I want Cartwright behind bars within the hour. I

will not stand for malversation. Anyone with any involvement with Cartwright's dirty practices will answer for their malfeasance."

"What do you want us to do about Chief Brown?" Reid asked.

"Get Cartwright to flip on the chief, and I'll give you your warrant. I want every last charge to stick. Same goes for the names on this list—I want every T crossed and every I dotted. This is by the book. We cannot bend the law by the slightest fraction. I want ironclad arrests." Fox opened a manila folder that'd been sitting on his desk, pulled several forms out, and plucked a gold pen from its perch on a marble stand. After signing his name with a flourish to the pages that included search warrants for Cartwright's home and office, he tucked the papers back into the folder and handed it to Mac. "Does anyone know if this has to do with Brown's daughter's disappearance?"

Mac shrugged. "Is it possible? Hell yeah. Do we know for sure? No."

"Keep me posted and be safe, detective."

"Thank you, your Honor."

I turned to Larry before I left and stuck out my hand. "Thank you."

"Don't thank me. I don't deserve it."

Larry was correct; he didn't deserve gratitude after

everything he'd done, but I still gave it. It was his testimony that sealed Cartwright's fate.

———

"Do you want to talk about Harper?" Reid asked on the drive to Cartwright's office.

I was beginning to regret my suggestion to drive my truck downtown and leave Reid's Rover at the judge's house. The last thing I wanted to do was talk about Harper.

Mistaking my silence for acceptance, Reid continued, "I talked to her before she left. She was determined to make things right with you. I hope you heard her out."

"I did."

"So you two are good?" he asked.

Were we good? That was the furthest thing to what we were.

"We're done," I told him.

I felt his eyes shooting daggers as I drove, but refused to take my eyes off the road and look at him. I knew what I'd find—disappointment.

"The fuck, Mac? Didn't she apologize?"

"Sure did."

"Enough of the two-word answers, asshole. What happened?"

"She came to my house, said what she had to say. I disagreed, then left."

"Your house? Don't you mean *our* house? You moved her ass in there. Fought to have her there as a matter-of-fact. Now because she made one mistake, that she tried to rectify, you're kicking her out and done with her?"

"No. We're done because she was right. I'm not the person she thought I was. She can't—actually, she shouldn't have to deal with my shit after everything she's been through."

"What do you mean you're not who she thought you were?" Reid pushed.

I didn't want to have this conversation. I needed to get Harper and my personal life out of my head and think about how we were going to arrest Cartwright.

Reid made a noise that sounded a lot like a growl and I wondered how pissed his wife would be if I dropped him off at the next red light and she had to come pick his stranded ass up?

"You know the things I've done," I answered.

"Are you talking about that shithead Jimmy?" he snarled. "That dirt-bag got exactly what he deserved. A bullet between his eyes. If you hadn't done it, I would've. Jimmy was a threat to my family. You were completely justified."

"Harper deserves better."

Why was this so hard for Reid to understand?

"Huh. So you think Ava deserves better than me? You know what I do. You know the things I've done."

"Of course not. I'm not you…"

Reid cut me off. "What the fuck does that mean?"

"Nothing. Can we stop talking about Harper, please? We're done."

"Yeah, we'll see."

I didn't bother asking Reid what he meant by that comment. We were pulling into the underground parking structure of The Hall of Justice where the DA's office was located, cutting off any further talk.

After the parking attendant waved us through with a flash of my shield, we parked and made our way to the bank of elevators—thankfully in silence.

"How are we playing this?" Reid asked as the elevator approached the floor we needed.

Shouldn't we have been talking about this on the drive over instead of my fucked-up love life? My jaw hurt from clenching my teeth, my head was pounding from thinking about Harper, and I was pissed as hell—at myself. My day had turned into shit. The only silver lining was Cartwright's reign of corruption would end today.

"Cuff him and haul his ass into one of the special operations interrogation rooms. We can live feed our interview to Judge Fox. By the time we're done here, Brown's warrant will be ready."

"You think it's a good idea to cuff him out in the open? We don't know who's working with Cartwright and Brown," Reid reminded me.

That was exactly why I had to get Harper out of my head. I almost screwed up.

"Shit. You're right. Someone could easily tip off Brown. We'll go in soft and ask him for a word in private."

The elevator opened and the man of the hour stood waiting outside the door with his detail in tow.

Perfect.

"Mr. District Attorney, you're the man I needed to see." I plastered a fake smile on my face and held my contempt in check the best I could.

Graham Cartwright wasn't worthy of the title district attorney and he certainly didn't warrant the courtesy of mister either. However, addressing him as Captain Douchebag of the Century wasn't going to get me a meeting with the man.

"Detective." Cartwright stepped to the side, allowing us to exit the elevator. "I'm on my way out. Did we have a meeting?"

"No. This won't take long but I have new information on Nicole Brown I think you're going to want immediately," I lied.

"Can you email it? I'm already running late."

I leaned in close and whispered, "You're gonna want to hear this now. I have exactly what you need to nail a few big-name players with life sentences. Including Jason Riggers."

Cartwright's eyes flared and he turned to his detail. "We'll leave in ten minutes." Then he turned back to us. "Follow me, we can use one of the SOI rooms. Right this way."

A brief walk and Cartwright pushed open an interrogation room door gesturing for us to precede him. At this point, it was hard to hold back my laugh. The asshole had happily walked himself to his own interrogation. When we entered, Reid immediately went to work closing the blinds. He set his laptop on the metal table and went to work connecting to the live feed Dustin had already set up.

"What happened to your leg?" I asked, noticing he was walking with a severe limp.

"Nothing. Pulled a muscle playing racquetball. What's this about Nicole?" Cartwright asked.

That was a lie. There was no chance Graham Cartwright played racquetball. It was doubtful the man had seen the inside of a gym in over thirty years.

"Sit down, Graham. Make yourself comfortable. We're gonna be here a while," I instructed, pulling out a chair and pointing at it.

The man's eyes narrowed. Maybe it was from my use of his first name, maybe it was because I had given him an order, maybe he didn't like my tone. I didn't know which of those things bothered him the most. What I did know was I didn't give the first fuck what he thought or how he felt.

"Excuse me?" he asked.

I watched as Reid stepped in front of the door with an unmasked smile.

"I'm sorry. Was I not clear? Have a seat. I have some questions for you regarding the Jason Riggers' case."

"Jason Riggers? You have questions for me?" he asked.

"Indeed. Let's start with the arrest warrant that was issued by Judge Barnes and we'll go from there."

"I don't have time for this, Detective Mackenzie, and I don't appreciate your tone. Do you have information about Nicole Brown's disappearance or not? Because it seems to me you're wasting time while a young girl's life is in danger."

"Okay. Let's talk about Nicole first. How do you know her life is in danger?"

"Detective, the girl was taken against her will. How is she not in danger?" Cartwright queried.

"How do you know she was taken against her will? Did you see something you haven't reported?"

Cartwright put his finger in the collar of his shirt, pulling the tight fabric away from his skin while he lifted his chin. His discomfort was rising.

"Why are you wasting my time with this bullshit?" he snapped and rubbed his injured leg.

"Bullshit? As you said, a woman's life may be in danger. How is discussing the case bullshit?"

Graham Cartwright had backed himself in a corner and was trying his damnedest not to show he was uncomfortable talking about Nicole. "Does Tom Brown know his friend arranged the kidnapping of his daughter?" I asked.

"I sincerely hope you are not insinuating what I think you are. I would think carefully before you make an inflammatory accusation to the district attorney."

"I'm not insinuating anything. I am asking you a direct question. Does Tom know you arranged to have his daughter kidnapped?"

"That's absurd. I did no such thing."

"See, I have proof you did. I know you've approached just about every person in the San Francisco underworld to renegotiate payouts, bribes, and protection fees. I know that Judge Barnes is one of many you have on your payroll. I know that you had Jason Riggers incarcerated for a crime you actually committed. You may not have been the one that beat Edward, but the man you hired has come forward. I know you railroaded Riggers because his MC refused to pay you off. You see, I've crawled so far up your ass, Cartwright, you won't be seeing the light of day for a very long time."

It was time to see if Cartwright would flip to save his own ass.

"Graham Cartwright, you're under arrest for..."

"What the fuck?" Cartwright started yelling before I could finish telling him his charges. He continued to yell profanities at me as I read him his Miranda rights.

"Do you understand the rights I have read to you?" I finished.

"I'm going to have your ass in a sling, you piece of shit!" Cartwright bellowed; however, there was less bluster.

"Wouldn't be the first time," Reid mumbled from his perch at the door.

"It's time to play let's make a deal," I told him.

The next two hours were nothing short of Cartwright lying, denying, and generally bullshitting me. I was tired. I had hoped not to have to play this card but time was running out. I needed to get to Brown. There was already a chance that he'd been tipped off. Sometime in the middle of the interrogation, Reid excused himself to call Austin and Dustin, asking his men to tail the police chief. There was some measure of reassurance someone had eyes on him, but that didn't mean we could listen in.

"You're going down, Cartwright. There are no ifs, ands, or buts about it. We have enough evidence for life without parole. You know how this works; I even gave you the courtesy of letting you listen to a snippet of one of the conversations. I'm not playing games with you. You're fucked. Brown, however, is going to pin everything on you and walk free."

"I don't know what the fuck you're talking about."

Same answer.

"Okay. We're done here. We're going to walk you out of here in cuffs, take you to central booking, and you'll be afforded a bond hearing in the morning. I hope you know what you're doing." I stood and collected the files I had on the desk, placing them in my messenger bag, and pulling out the last file I'd been saving. Blaze had hand-delivered it to Reid earlier. A piece of information that Damion had gathered on Cartwright years ago. The last thing that he'd want coming out. Damion had been able to hang it over Graham's head for years.

I looked over at Reid to make sure he'd already severed the connection to Judge Fox and closed his laptop. I didn't want this last piece of information broadcasted.

"One more thing before we go." I leaned in and

lowered my voice. "There's the matter of Katrina Cartwright." I opened the file and let the images fall to the table. The photographs were crystal clear and no denying the man in the pictures was Graham Cartwright. He was clearly catching his wife's car on fire. The male driver was badly injured and unconscious but Katrina was awake. Several images showed her panicked expression while Cartwright poured gasoline all over the car. I moved the images around the table, making sure he got a good look at the most grotesque. Katrina on fire, her alive and burning, and finally her burnt body at the morgue.

"Can you still smell it, Graham? If you inhale real deep, is the stench of Katrina's burning flesh still infused in your nostrils?"

"Where? How? What do you want?" Cartwright jerked in his chair, his eyes finally meeting mine.

"Talk. I want everything you have on Tom Brown and this file goes back to where it's been locked all these years, never seeing the inside of a courtroom."

He seemed to be contemplating his next words carefully. "I want your word that Remy never sees those pictures." Gone was the defiant district attorney, he was crestfallen and knew he was defeated. "I'll give you what you need on Tom Brown."

Over the course of an hour, Cartwright told a story that was so deep and colored in corruption I wondered what good, if any, I actually did as a police officer. Shakedowns, collusion with local gangs, drug sales, prostitution, you name it Chief Brown was involved. With the Fivers moving into the city, the chief's income had greatly increased. Brown didn't feel like sharing a dirty pay raise with Cartwright. In his greed, he went out on his own and tried to undercut Brown.

No honor among thieves.

25

POLICE OFFICER SHOT

Harper

"Have you heard from them?" I asked Ava.

"Not since the last time you called. All Reid said was that he was busy and wouldn't be home until late," she answered.

"Have you and the kids eaten?" I asked.

"No, we haven't." She laughed. "Settle down. Everything is okay."

It wasn't okay. I could feel it in my bones. Something was way, way, wrong. Not that I would tell Ava that and freak her out. I hated that Mac left the house mad, but that wasn't it. There was a pain, an actual physical pain, in my chest. It felt like someone had punched me between my collarbone and heart.

"I'll bring Chinese over. Call in the order to China House."

Ava still hadn't stopped laughing at me, no doubt she'd thought I'd lost my mind. "Okay. I'll see you soon."

We clicked off and I grabbed my purse. I had to get out of the house. I'd been pacing for hours, replaying the last nine months of my life. Everything I could remember.

When I first met Mac at Del Mar's, I was so jealous when I thought that Mac was Ava's man. The first time he came in after I started working there he sat at the counter ordering a coffee, after giving her a hug and a kiss on the cheek. He asked about JJ and if there was anything she needed done around the house. One time he even took her car for an oil change. Ava was stuck at work and couldn't take it in herself. Ten minutes later in walks Mac, trades her keys, and with a kiss to the cheek he leaves. All I could think about was how desperately I wanted a man like that. Someone who would happily help; even if it was something inconvenient, like sitting at a garage waiting on an oil change.

Then I met Reid. He started coming in with Mac in the mornings and having breakfast at the counter, chatting with Ava as she rushed by. That's when I became over-the-moon jealous. But not of her and Mac, or even her and Reid. It was because the man couldn't look in her direction without eating her up with his eyes. There was no denying that Logan Reid was hot for Ava Kelley. Reid would move heaven and hell for Ava. There was no hiding it from anyone—except Ava. She walked around the café completely oblivious that Reid was in love with her. It was fun to watch the two of them dance around each other. Reid was gentle and slow with her, always cautious of her limitations. The opposite of Mac. Once Reid had stepped up and claimed Ava and JJ, Mac changed tactics with Ava and pushed her to move on from Jacob's death. He was relentless in making her accept that it was time to start living again.

It was somewhere in all of Ava's trouble that I fell in love with Mac. He was fierce and loyal. There was nothing he wasn't willing to do for two people he loved most, even at his own peril. I knew it was hurting Mac when Ava pushed him away, but he refused to let up. He wanted both of them happy and in the end, I believe it was because Mac had pushed Ava so hard that she was able to commit to opening herself and JJ up to Reid.

Luckily, China House was quick getting our food together because the longer I sat in the restaurant waiting the more my chest started burning. I spent the drive to Ava's trying to get my mind off my pain and started thinking about the first time I saw Mac in Stripes. It was the first time I'd been to a BDSM club.

I'd walked around looking at all the different roped off areas. Each one had its own specialized equipment for play. As I roamed the large room, my emotions had ranged from hell no to hell yes. There was so much I wanted to try but my brain won out and in the end, I remembered that taking on a Dom wasn't something that I could rush. I needed to be safe and sane, something I didn't have time for. I was never in one place long enough to cultivate that type of relationship. As I was leaving, Mac stopped me. My surprise quickly changed into embarrassment. I was horrified he'd seen me in a kink club until I remembered he was there, too, looking for the same thing I was—a play partner. At the time I thought Mac was the answer. He was safe. Boy, was I wrong. The man was lethal. With a look, a smile, and a swat of his hand, the man could bring me to my knees. I tried to fight every feelings I had for him. I couldn't get involved and I certainly couldn't commit. Eventually, I'd have to leave. The longer our relationship went on, the harder I knew it'd be to go, but I didn't stop it. Being with Mac made me feel human. When we were together, he made me forget I had a bounty on my head. I didn't have to think when he was around. He demanded I didn't. All I had to do was be.

By the time I pulled up to Ava's, I was ready to come out of my skin. I needed to talk to Mac. I needed to hear his voice.

The kids greeted me at the door with smiles and exuberance that only children possess, pulling the first ounce of happiness from me since this morning.

"Hi, Auntie Harper. Mama got me new hair bands. Do you want to see them?" Melody bounced in excitement, barely giving me enough room to walk in the door.

"Geez, Melly, let her in the door. Do you need help?" JJ asked.

"Thank you, JJ." I smiled down at the young man and handed him a bag. He was becoming more and more like Mac and Reid every day—thoughtful and considerate. "And yes, Melly, I'd love to see your new hair bows after dinner."

"Okay." Melody hopped ahead of us.

"Mom said she'd be right down," JJ informed me and led us into the kitchen. "She's on the phone."

Oh, God. I hoped she was talking to Reid. If I didn't hear something new soon, I was going to track them down myself.

"Hey," Ava said as she joined us in the kitchen.

"Everything okay?" I quickly asked.

"Yes. That was Suzie. She's still getting the hang of the produce order. Running the café is harder than she thought."

Suzie had been doing a great job since she took over the day-to-day operations of the café, but helping with the back-end part of owning a restaurant and having to do it by yourself was very different.

"Does she need more help?" I asked and passed out the takeout containers.

"No, she's figuring it out and Michael is helping a lot. I think he's going to take an early retirement."

Suzie's husband, Michael, was a police officer, too. He didn't work at Mac's station anymore but he had worked with both Mac and Jacob early in his career.

"Any reason why?" I asked. Michael was a little older than Mac but I didn't think he was anywhere near the age of retirement.

"Michael says that there's a different feel around the city. He doesn't enjoy being a cop anymore. He also mentioned that morale among the cops, especially the ones that have been there a while, is at an all-time low."

"Has Mac said anything about it?" I asked Ava. I tried to remember if he'd said anything to me about problems at the station, but I couldn't remember if he had.

"Not to me. Reid said there were rumors floating around about some trouble with the chief, but he didn't elaborate. Then there's Nicole Brown. She's been missing like three-ish weeks now. There used to be a code that even a criminal lived by—no families. But not anymore. I'm happy Michael is getting out."

"Mac did talk to me about Nicole. How scary. I can't believe she hasn't been found yet."

The kids happily dug into their food. Melly giggled at something her brother said and I realized how desperately I wanted that. I wanted kids sitting around the dinner table laughing. I wanted bedtimes and stories. I wanted to see Mac with a pretty little girl and a handsome boy. I wanted to watch Mac as he taught our children to grow up and be mini versions of himself.

"You okay? You totally spaced out there for a minute," Ava whispered.

"Yea. No. I don't know. I don't like how things were left with Mac before he was called out. He's still really mad at me. He wouldn't budge; just kept saying we were done."

"Give him a minute, he's stubborn and hotheaded. He loves you, I know he does. There's no way you two are done."

"I hope you're right."

"I know I am. Let's go sit with the kids," she suggested.

The rest of dinner was spent with JJ and Melly entertaining us with their stories from school. JJ was quite the ladies' man. Apparently, four girls from his class had tried to kiss him on the playground, which he declared was gross. Melly had a new best friend. A boy named Leon. Leon was short for some name she couldn't remember but promised it was the coolest name ever and she was naming her next boy doll after him.

The kids had been dismissed from the table to go watch TV, the kitchen had been cleaned, and Ava was making a fresh pot of coffee. Probably sensing I wasn't leaving anytime soon and she'd need the caffeine to stay awake and entertain my crazy paranoia. I was staring out the big window from the breakfast nook enjoying the view of the Bay Bridge lit up when all the fine hairs at the base of my neck started to tingle.

You know when you get a sixth sense, something that you can't explain but you know to be true? That's what was happening. The pain in my chest sharpened and I thought I might be sick.

"Mom. The TV said there was a police officer shot!" JJ yelled from the kitchen.

The clatter of something hitting the floor made me turn. Ava was staring at me, unmoving.

"Daddy says to turn the channel. We're not allowed to watch that," Melly said.

"Stop, Melody," JJ demanded and after a beat, he continued, "I think I saw Dad."

That got Ava moving. She ran into the living room, leaving me standing in the nook. I rubbed the ache in my chest and I knew.

Ava's phone rang and I heard her start to cry. There was a series of short clipped answers before she came back into the kitchen.

"Harper."

I didn't answer her.

"Honey, we have to go."

I still couldn't find my voice.

"It's Mac. He's been shot."

I knew.

The pain intensified as my own heart broke. I was losing him.

26

THE UNKNOWN

Reid

The coppery smell of blood was thick in the back of the ambulance, making me want to gag, but that's not what had my attention. It was her small, able hands. The purple latex gloves she wore were covered in Mac's blood. The contrast was morbid. She cleaned and packed his wound with practiced efficiency. Slow and methodical as if Mac's life wasn't literally in her hands. As soon as Mac was loaded into the back of the rig, the female medic removed the mask she'd been using to force air into his lungs, replacing it with something akin to a long-handled plastic cooking spoon she inserted down Mac's throat. I was now sitting beside him, watching his blood spill faster than she could stop it.

I heard the woman utter a small curse under her

breath as she ripped open another sterile package of gauze.

"You can talk to him," she told me.

"Huh?"

"Talk to him," she semi-repeated. This time it wasn't a suggestion, it was more a demand.

Fuck. What was there to say? Why did you step in front of me? Thanks for taking a bullet for me? What the hell were you thinking? What was I going to tell Ava? Harper?

Jesus Christ!

There was nothing to say. Should I yell at him not to die? Beg him to hold on? All the words were caught in my throat as I prayed the requests I couldn't verbalize.

A monitor beeped, making me flinch as I blinked the tears from my eyes. That should be me. I should be the one dying on the gurney, not Mac.

"Thank you," I whispered to Mac. "Hold tight, brother, we're almost there. You'll be patched up in no time."

"This is Galloway, Unit 15, en route to San Francisco General, thirty-nine-year-old male, GSW to chest, no exit wound observed. LMA inserted, patient is unconscious, hypovolemic shock, ETA three minutes."

"Three minutes, Mac, you hold on. Please, God, brother, hold on."

"He's doing great," Galloway told me, still holding pressure on Mac's chest.

"He doesn't look great," I muttered.

"He's alive. That's what matters right now. One minute, one step at a time."

One minute at a time. I wasn't sure if I could do that, not when each second felt like an eternity. With each rotation of the ambulance's tires, it felt like we were inching toward Mac's death.

"Have you done this before?" she asked.

"Huh?"

"Ridden in the back of a rig?"

"Yes."

"So you understand what's going to happen when we will pull in and the doors open? The team will be waiting for us. Get out, step aside, and answer any questions you can. If you don't know, say you don't know."

Before I could remind her I knew what was going to happen, the doors to the ambulance were thrown open and all hell broke loose. Mac was pulled from the back, the wheels of the gurney magically appearing. Galloway was out and the team of doctors were on the move.

I jumped out and had to hurry to catch up.

Galloway was getting the doctors up to speed on Mac's condition, her partner coming up to meet us while adding in details.

A man who looked like he was in need of a haircut shook my arm to get my attention. "Are you with him? Do you know him well?"

"Um, yeah. He's a friend," I answered, still in a daze.

"Great. I'm Dr. Matthews, the anesthesiologist. Is he allergic to anything?"

"No—not that I know of."

"Any medical conditions? Is he taking any medications, vitamins?"

"No conditions, no medications, I don't know about vitamins or supplements."

"All right. Thanks," the doctor said and rushed to Mac's side.

"Bed space 1," an older doctor called as we approached the exam areas in the ER. The gurney was pushed in and came to a stop next to a hospital bed. "On three. One... two... three."

A team of nurses and doctors moved Mac to the bed and Galloway quickly pulled the ambulance gurney out of the way.

"Step out here with me for a moment. Give them some space," she suggested.

I followed her a few feet away and watched in a

weird disconnected way as the doctors and nurses connected Mac up to so many machines my eyes couldn't track fast enough.

"Dr. Matthews is the Chief of Anesthesiology. His reputation is stellar. Dr. Coats is a trauma surgeon that practiced at Maryland's Shock Trauma for twenty years before coming here. If that was me in there, I'd want Dr. Coats and her team working on me. Your friend is in critical condition, but this is the best place in the city. Is there anyone you need to call?"

I looked down at Galloway, noting how calm yet assertive she'd been throughout arriving on the scene and pushing me aside, taking over, giving Mac CPR to delivering him here to the hospital. She was competent and reassuring, someone I'd want on my team.

"Reid?" Her voice pulled me from my thoughts.

"My team already called my wife. They went to go pick her up. Thank you," I answered.

"Good. He'll be going up in a minute, to the tenth floor for surgery, there's a waiting room up there."

"Thank you for everything, Galloway. You and your partner."

"Just doing..."

"Don't say that. Not to me. I use that same line when a victim thanks me. You and I both know what it takes out of you. Each call you answer, each new patient, the risk, the unknown. It may be your job, but you give a piece of yourself every time you get in that rig. Thank you for that. Thank you for saving his life."

Galloway pursed her lips and looked away. "You're welcome."

"Jen, you ready? We got another call-out," her partner said as he rushed past us.

"Damn."

"Seems to be a busy night. Go."

With a smile and a nod, she was gone.

JJ

Mom was crying and hugging Aunt Harper while Dad, Austin, and Dustin kept walking back and forth in front of them. Melly was squeezing my hand so hard it hurt, but I tried not to show it. My sister needed me.

"Jakey?" she whispered.

"Yeah."

"Can you ask your daddy to make Uncle Mac better?"

"What do you mean? Dad already explained that Uncle Mac was getting the bullet out and he's fighting really hard," I tried to remind her without crying. I was eleven now. Eleven-year-old boys aren't supposed to cry anymore. But it was really hard.

"No. Your daddy Jacob in heaven. Please, Jakey.

You have to ask him. Mommy says that it's okay when I talk to my mommy in heaven. But my mommy didn't know Uncle Mac. Your daddy did. They were like best friends. Your daddy can help him."

Mom still took Melly to the cemetery so she could talk to her mom. She was buried next to my dad Jacob. Sometimes I went with them so I could visit with my dad but most the time I let them go alone. Dad says that it's good that I take care of our girls and know when they need time together. I wasn't sure what that meant but when they went, me and Dad got time alone. I liked that. I liked when we did cool things.

"I'll ask him," I told her.

"Thank you, Jakey. I'm so scared."

"Me, too."

Melly crawled onto my lap and cried into my shoulder. Dad looked at me, his face tight, and he gave me a lift of his chin. He liked that I was taking care of my sister. Uncle Mac had to be okay, I couldn't lose him, too.

***

Ava

I was trying to be strong but I was failing. Mac had to be okay. The day he came to the house and told me Jacob had been shot was playing on a loop in my head.

How Mac looked when I broke down in his arms. How the pain of loss took my breath away and I thought I'd be crippled for the rest of my life. How Mac and Reid put me back together. He had to pull through. Had to!

Reid

It'd been five goddamned hours since Mac went back for surgery. A nurse had come out a few hours ago to give us an update. *Still in surgery but doing better than expected.*

That was it.

Melody had fallen asleep in JJ's lap and had been moved to a bank of chairs where she could comfortably sleep, leaving JJ to sit with Ava and Harper. My boy was trying his best to be brave. He had hugged his sister when she cried and was now holding his mom's hand with a strength that no boy should have. But, damn, I was proud of him. Mac would be, too.

Mac.

"Come here, little man."

JJ let go of Ava's hand and walked to me. I knelt down in front of him and tagged him around the back of his neck, bringing his forehead to mine.

"Proud of you, son. You're being brave and strong

for our girls, but it's okay to be worried. I know this is hard on you."

JJ didn't speak right away. This was something he'd started recently. When he had something important to say, he'd stop and think, gathering his thoughts before he spoke.

"I'm scared."

"I know you are. I'm scared, too."

"You are?" JJ sounded shocked at my admission.

"Of course I am."

"I don't want Mac to die. Melly asked me to talk to my dad." JJ pressed his lips together, then began again. "You know, my dad in heaven, to ask him to help Uncle Mac." The tears I needed to see started to fall. "I asked him. I'm so scared Uncle Mac is going to die, too."

"Son, look at me." I waited for his tear-filled eyes to look up and continued, "First, you never be ashamed and look away when you're showing emotion for someone you love. It's okay to cry. It's okay to yell. It's okay to be scared. While you're learning how to grow up and take care of those you love, you remember part of that is you being honest with them, giving them your emotions, showing them how you feel. You're always safe to give me your pain, Jacob. As for your dad—you never, and I repeat never, be afraid to talk to your dad and ask him for his help. Your dad is a part of you, a part of your mom, and a part of our family. You don't think I talk to your dad, too?"

"You do?" JJ asked.

"Yeah, little man, I do. I talk to your dad all the time. I ask him for guidance in raising you to be the man he would want you to be. I ask him to watch out for you and your mom when you're away from me. And tonight, I've begged your dad to watch over Mac."

"I think you're raising me to be the man he would want me to be. Because I'm learning how to be like you and Uncle Mac. And dad was like you, and Uncle Mac. So, I guess I'm growing up to be like him, too."

"Damn right." I squeezed the back of his neck. "You good, son?"

"I'm good, Dad."

"Good. Now go sit back with your mom. I need to talk to Harper."

JJ pulled me in for a hug and whispered in my ear, "I love you, Dad."

"I love you."

I pulled all the strength I could from JJ and set out to have a much-needed talk with Harper.

I'd been putting it off for hours now, but it was time for me to face the music.

27

WE'RE GOOD, BROTHER

"Image guidance, stat."

"Two more units of blood."

"I'm in."

The voices had stopped and the warmth had returned, pulling Mac back to his unconscious state. The memories of the shooting ran through his subconscious as if he was reliving them in vivid recollection.

The drive from the Hall of Justice to Chief Brown's home was spent going over the information Cartwright had given Mac and Reid. Once Cartwright was handed over to the Chief of Special Investigations and his team to be taken to central booking, the two men left to pick up Tom Brown.

A quick call to Austin told them that the chief was at home. He'd been there for the last hour after a meeting with a local gang leader in a shady part of the city that was rundown and mostly abandoned. It seemed Brown was neither careful nor smart about where he was seen.

"How do you think this is gonna go?" Reid asked Mac as they made their way across town.

"Tom Brown is a cocky son-of-a-bitch. He'll be pissed as shit at the implication of wrongdoing. My guess? He'll laugh it off, then he's going to rage and threaten us. His power has gone to his head; he thinks he's above the law," Mac mused.

"That's my thought, too. He's going to be a douche and say; *do you know who you're fucking with?* Or something equally jacked."

Tom Brown answered the door, not looking one bit surprised the men were there. His suit jacket was off, but his shoulder holster was still on and his service weapon on full display.

"Detective, what can I do for you?" the police chief greeted.

"I have information about your daughter. May we come in?" Mac asked.

He didn't need to ask; he had a warrant that approved his entrance without permission. However, with Brown armed, it was better to go soft and get Brown contained before he mentioned that his days as police chief were over.

"Certainly."

Tom stepped aside, allowing both men to enter; however, before Mac could begin, Brown did. "It seems you've had a busy afternoon."

Fuck.

Two officers that Mac knew from the station stepped into view, both armed, both pointing weapons in their direction.

"You don't want to do this. Whether we walk out of here with you today or not, you're done. The feds have everything they need to take you down." Mac looked over to the cops and added, "You really wanna add murder charges to your sheet? Brown isn't gonna take the fall for this. You two are. He's gonna pin everything on you."

Brown laughed, throwing his head back, giving Mac and Reid the distraction they needed.

The draw of the gun, the aim, the trigger pull, the recoil of the pistol—it was second nature to the men. It was smooth, fluid, and accurate. Both police officers fell to the floor lifeless.

Mac turned to Brown as he leveled his weapon in Reid's direction. Without thought or concern for his own safety, Mac shoved Reid aside.

The burn of the bullet sliced through Mac, bringing him to his knees before he slumped to his side and clutched his chest.

There was another weapon discharged before Reid was forefront in Mac's line of sight.

"Jesus Christ!" Reid yelled. "Hold on, brother, help is on the way."

Mac tried to talk but he couldn't breathe deep enough to get the words out. The pain dulled and the roaring in his ears lessened.

"Mac! Stay awake."

"We're good, brother." Mac hoped Reid could hear him. "Take care of them."

Mac was losing the battle, his lids were heavy, and his breathing was slowing.

Everything was going to be okay. Reid would take care of Ava, JJ, and Melody. They would all pull Harper into the fold and make sure she was safe.

"Tell Harper... tell her I love her."

"He's coding."

"Get the paddles."

"Clear."

"Again."

28

BLAME GAME

Harper

"Let's take a walk."

Reid pulled me from my thoughts of Mac and held his hand out to me.

I didn't bother answering since he wasn't asking, I just took his hand and let him pull me up from the chair I'd been sulking in for hours. I was grateful for his help standing; with each minute that ticked by, I was becoming less and less certain that Mac would make it.

Once we were in the hall and the door to the waiting room had clicked shut, Reid turned to me with more devastation across his features than I'd ever seen —on anyone.

"It's my fault."

"What is?" I asked.

"Mac being shot. He took that bullet for me. Before I could stop him, Mac pushed me out of the way and caught one in the chest. I should be the one in surgery, not him."

I swallowed the saliva that had flooded my mouth, washing the bile back down my throat. I'd asked Reid what'd happened hours ago. He'd refused to tell me even though I'd begged. He kept telling me that we needed to concentrate on the present—one minute at a time. Now I knew why. It should've been Reid, not Mac. I pressed on my chest where the ache still hadn't subsided and looked back at Reid. He should be the one fighting for his life. The anger that was bubbling up was squelched when I thought about Ava and their kids. If it'd been Reid, then JJ and Melly would be even more worried than they are now. Ava didn't deserve to have two men that she loved die. And the more I thought about it, the more I remembered who Mac was —loyal, protective, honorable. I was a selfish bitch for even allowing anger to creep into my mind.

"Of course he did. You're his best friend, his brother." I squared my shoulders and tried my hardest to be what Reid had said I was—strong. Strong enough to be Mac's woman. "I wouldn't expect anything less of him. It's not your fault. You didn't shoot him."

"Did you hear me, Harper? He pushed me out of the way."

"I heard you. What I don't understand is why you're so surprised. Did you not think Mac was brave enough to take a bullet for you? I've heard him tell Ava he'd protect you with his life. Did you think he was a liar?"

"Fuck no."

"Then stop. Mac doesn't need us playing the blame game; he needs us to stay strong for him. When he comes out of surgery, he's going to need all of us. Especially you. You can't feel guilty or be pissed at him. We'll get through this together, like a family. It's what he needs. And it's damn well what he's going to get."

"I knew I was right." Reid smiled.

"About what?"

"I knew you had a strength in you that is exactly what Mac needs. We're all here for you, anything you need."

"Thank you."

Reid pulled me in for a hug and I lost control of the tears I was holding back.

"Let it out, Harper. There is no use trying to hold everything in."

I did what Reid suggested and I let go. At some point, Reid carried me to a nearby chair and sat down with me in his lap. I was thankful that no one else was there to witness my breakdown and more than grateful that Reid cushioned the pain just a little for me. But more than anything, I wished I was in Mac's arms.

***

"AIDEN MACKENZIE'S FAMILY?" an older woman asked as she walked into the waiting room.

"Yes." Reid stood.

I stayed cemented in place, too afraid to move.

"I'm Dr. Coats. Aiden is in ICU. I was able to get the bullet..."

The woman's mouth continued to move but I could no longer hear what she was saying. Mac was alive. He made it. That was the only information that was important to me. The rest? Unimportant details. All I needed to know was that Mac was breathing. We'd work through the rest later.

"... one at a time."

"Harper goes first," Ava said.

"What?"

"He can have one visitor. You go. We'll wait here."

I was on autopilot as I followed the doctor to Mac's room. It was a miracle I made it without collapsing.

I stood outside the glass doors and stared in at all the machines Mac was hooked up to.

"It looks scarier than it is. He's still intubated, the sound you can hear whooshing is the ventilator. It keeps the oxygen flowing through his body. The beeping you hear is the ECG, it is monitoring his heart rate. And every so often you'll hear the blood pressure cuff activate and take a reading. When you go in, I'll turn down the ECG monitor."

"No, leave it," I told her. "I want to hear his heart beating."

"Very well. You can sit with him and touch him, hold his hand if you wish. Be careful not to disconnect any of his leads, but other than that you're free to move around."

"Thank you."

When I entered the room, the beeps became noticeably louder and the whooshing sound the doctor had described was distinct and reassuring.

I sat next to Mac and picked up his hand, surprised at how warm it was. If I closed my eyes and blocked out the hospital sounds, I could almost believe he was simply sleeping.

"I love you. I don't know if you can hear me but I love you so much." I brought my lips down to kiss his knuckles and rested my cheek there.

"Don't leave me, Mac. I don't know what led me to this city and to you, but I do know you are exactly who I was always meant to be with. I can't say goodbye. You have to be okay. Just hold on."

I touched the soreness in my chest, relieved the

pain was still there. As long as I felt the ache, that meant Mac was still alive.

"I feel it. In my chest. I felt it before I knew. It hurts, Mac."

The monitors beeped, the ventilator whooshed, and I prayed.

29

IT HURTS

"It hurts, Mac."

Mac stared down at his wife lying in the hospital bed and thought she'd never looked more beautiful, more radiant than she did at that moment. Not the day he married her, not on their honeymoon when she pranced around in her bikini, not any of the times he'd taken her. Right now, at this moment, pregnant with his children, she was spectacular.

"I know it does, baby. Just a little longer. You're doing great." Mac kissed her forehead and tried to distract her. "We have to decide on names."

Harper smiled, knowing what he was doing. "I already decided."

"And? Are you going to tell me what my babies' names are?" he teased.

Over the last six months, they had made a list of

possible names for the twins. They ranged from same first letters, rhyming names, old-fashioned, unique to plain. The list had grown and grown. What hadn't happened was a final decision. Mac didn't much care what names Harper picked for their first names, all that mattered to him was their last names, they were Mackenzies.

"Matthew Robert and Madison Jane," she told him.

"So we're going with the M theme, huh?"

"We are. I want to name him after your dad. If he gets an M, she needs one, too."

"Whatever you want."

Mac smiled at his wife and knew his life was perfect. He had more beauty than any one man should be allowed. The longer he looked at Harper, the hazier she became; he slowly blinked his eyes, trying to restore his vision. When he did, his head pounded in excruciating pain and a blinding light shining in his face caused him to clench his lids closed and recoil from the source.

"Mac!" He could hear Harper crying but couldn't open his eyes to find her.

"Don't fight it," another voice said.

Harper. Where was Harper? Were his babies okay?

"Everyone out."

His last thoughts were of his wife before the bright late faded and he was plunged into darkness.

"He'll wake up when he's ready."

"It's been days. I thought he was going to open his eyes. He was fighting so hard," Harper cried.

"His body is healing. Everything looks great. Just be patient."

"I'm trying." I wanted to smile at the impatience in Harper's tone. "He squeezed my hand."

"That's normal. His brain is still functioning, sending—"

"No. I mean, he squeezed it. He didn't twitch. Mac, can you hear me?"

Of course, I could hear her. I tried to answer but found I couldn't swallow.

"He did it again. He squeezed."

"Harper, slow down. Let it happen naturally."

"Okay. Please open your eyes, Mac," she whispered.

That's my girl. She didn't know the meaning of slow.

My eyelid was pulled open and a blinding light replaced the darkness.

Christ.

I tried to jerk my head away and forced my heavy eyelids to open, coming face-to-face with a woman I'd never seen before and the offending flashlight.

"Welcome back, Aiden. I am Dr. Coats. You're in San Francisco General Hospital. You need to stay calm. Blink your eyes if you understand."

I tried to do what the doctor asked but the need to swallow was too great. I was choking.

"No, Aiden. Stop. You have a breathing tube in. I'm going to remove it but you have to remain calm."

Fuck calm, I had to swallow.

"Mac. Please stay still."

Harper. Her voice washed over me and I willed myself to beat back the need to breathe. Anything for her.

"Very good. I'm going to remove the tube now. There will be lots of pulling when it comes out but you'll be able to breathe on your own. Don't fight it. Deep breath when it's out."

Pulling? Is that what the doctor called a fucking five-foot snake being yanked out of your throat?

I inhaled and wished the tube was still in - it hurt so bad to breathe. A thousand needles pierced my lungs and scraped my throat.

"Harper," I strained.

"Don't try to talk," the doctor said and placed a plastic mask over my mouth.

I reached up to remove it when Harper grabbed my hand, stopping me.

"Relax. I'm not going anywhere. We have all the time in the world."

I settled back into the bed and kept my eyes on Harper while the doctor continued her exam. Soon the room was filled with more staff. Through it all, it was Harper's smile that calmed me. I couldn't take my eyes off her.

"When do I get to leave?" I asked no one in particular.

Reid, Ava, and Harper were all sitting in my room. Austin and Dustin had left a little while ago, taking JJ and Melody with them.

"Dude. You've been awake about ten hours after being shot, in a coma, and almost dying. I'd say you're gonna be here a while longer." Reid laughed.

Yeah. Real funny. He wasn't the one in the bed hooked up to a thousand monitors that beeped constantly. He wasn't the one getting scans and blood drawn. I was worried that the next test the doctor-of-torture would require a scope up my ass. At this point, a rectal exam was all that was left.

"Harper, do you need anything before we leave?" Ava asked.

"No. I'm fine. Thank you."

I should've told Harper it was okay to go home. Reid told me she hadn't left the hospital once since I was brought in and she nearly took Austin's head off when he told her she needed to go get some sleep. But I wasn't. I was a selfish prick and too scared to let her out of my sight. I had been a dick to her before I was shot. What if she'd listened to me and had moved out already? We hadn't had a chance to talk in private yet, and until I made sure she knew how sorry I was and how much I loved her, she was staying put.

"Alright, then. We'll let you two rest." Ava stood and walked to the side of the bed. Tears filled her eyes as she looked down at me.

"I'm fine. Promise. You can't get rid of me that easy." I laughed.

"Don't joke about that, Aiden. I don't know what any of us would've done if we lost you," she said.

"Ava. I'm fine."

She gave me a nod of her head and moved into Reid's arms. "We'll catch you tomorrow." Reid was silent for a minute, then cleared his throat. "Can't thank you enough, brother. You saved my life. We both know it. Glad you're okay."

I swallowed the lump in my throat. When I saw

Brown lift his gun in Reid's direction, all I could see was JJ. He'd already lost one dad in his short life, I couldn't let him lose Reid, too.

They finished up their goodbyes, leaving Harper and me alone for the first time. I wasn't entirely sure how to start the conversation that needed to be had. Luckily, I didn't have to start it. Harper did.

"I didn't pack my stuff," she said.

"Okay."

"I'm not moving out."

"Okay."

"And you're not leaving me. I'm not letting you. We can work through anything. But you're not breaking up with me. Why are you smiling?" she huffed.

"Because I love you. Because you are so much smarter than I am. And because you are cute as hell when you're bossy."

"Well, get used to it because while you're recovering I'm in charge."

"Should I call you Mistress?" I laughed.

"Laugh all you want, Aiden, but I'm serious."

"I know you are."

She was more than cute when she was being bossy, she was sexy. The thought of calling her Mistress made my cock jerk, surprising the hell out of me. I'd never considered myself a switch but thinking about her in charge in the bedroom was stirring something inside of me. Not that I'd allow it for very long, but for the time being it would be amusing.

Mistress Harper.

"I love you. Thank you for being here even after I was a dick and didn't deserve it."

"I love you, too. There's no place else I'd be."

Harper settled back into the chair next to the bed and switched on the TV.

"This is Gloria Styles, Channel 9, with breaking news." A reporter announced, standing in front of what looked like the 501 precinct. "This is one of our darkest days as a city. The officers of the 501 were evacuated after rioters threw fire bombs into the lower windows, successfully catching the building on fire." The camera panned, showing what could only be described as a war zone in front of the station. Cars were on fire, police in full riot gear tried to push the crowd away from the steps of the 501. Men and women of all ages were throwing things and yelling in the background. "There's a convenience store across the street that has been looted and set on fire as well. The National Guard has been mobilized and a city-wide curfew is now in place. We just got word from the newsroom that all ground reporters and their crews have been recalled back to the station. It is no longer safe to be out here. Again, San Francisco is now in a state of emergency with an estimated thirty percent on fire. This is Gloria Styles for Channel 9 News. Please stay indoors and safe San Francisco."

The broadcast continued with aerial footage of the greater San Francisco area. I couldn't believe what I was seeing. The reporter hadn't been exaggerating. From the view high above the city buildings, it looked like a scene from a movie.

San Francisco was burning.

"Holy shit," I mumbled.

"You can say that again."

The hospital landline rang, jolting me from the television. Harper reached over and answered.

"He's right here. Hold on."

Harper maneuvered the phone cord so it would reach the bed without me having to move. I figured Reid had just seen the news broadcast as well. Shit. I hoped they were able to make it home safely.

"Hello?"

"Detective," Nico greeted.

My eyes shot to Harper, and she smiled and sat back down. Grabbing my hand, she went back to watching the news.

"I'm glad you're not dead," he said.

"Yeah. Me, too. Is that why you called?"

"Yes. That and to tell you that we're square. This is where you and I part ways."

Relief washed over me. Nico was honoring our agreement. Before I let him go, there was one last thing I needed to know.

"Tom Brown is dead," I told him.

"I heard, but not before he drilled one in you."

On cue, my chest started to burn, reminding me that Tom Brown did indeed almost kill me.

"His debt has been paid. I trust you'll do the right thing."

There was silence on the line and I thought he'd hung up on me.

"I'll text you."

I handed the phone back to Harper and she replaced the receiver back on the base. Before she could sit back down, I tugged her toward me.

"Lie with me."

"No way. I'll hurt you."

"Not a chance. The only thing that hurts is not having you in my arms."

"Okay. But if it starts to hurt, you promise to tell me?"

"Promise."

Not a chance.

Harper climbed in bed next to me, tossing her arm over my stomach and settled in.

Perfect.

Thank God, I hadn't lost her.

I had everything a man could ever need curled up in my arms and I was never letting go.

"I love you, Harper."

"Love you, Aiden."

"Had the craziest dream, or maybe it was a premonition," I told her.

"While you were in a coma?"

"Yeah."

"Will you tell me about it?"

"One day, after it comes true."

Harper snuggled in close and I breathed her in and the beauty she brought to my life. My future. I couldn't wait to hold those babies she was going to give me in my arms. As soon as I was out of here, I was marrying Harper. The children I'd dreamt of would be here soon if I had anything to say about it.

ALSO BY RILEY EDWARDS

Riley Edwards

www.RileyEdwardsRomance.com

Romantic Suspense

Red Team

Nightstalker

Protecting Olivia - Susan Stoker Universe

Redeeming Violet - Susan Stoker Universe

Recovering Ivy - Susan Stoker Universe

Rescuing Erin - Susan Stoker Universe

Romancing Rayne - Susan Stoker Universe

The Gold Team

Brooks - Susan Stoker Universe

The 707 Freedom Series

Free

Freeing Jasper

Finally Free

Freedom

The Next Generation (707 spinoff)

Saving Meadow

Chasing Honor

Finding Mercy

Claiming Tuesday

The Collective

Unbroken 1 & 2 – Season One

Trust – Season Two

ALSO BY RILEY EDWARDS

Romantic Suspense

Red Team

Nightstalker

Protecting Olivia - Susan Stoker Universe

Redeeming Violet - Susan Stoker Universe

Recovering Ivy - Susan Stoker Universe

Rescuing Erin - Susan Stoker Universe

Romancing Rayne - Susan Stoker FanFic

The Gold Team

Brooks - Susan Stoker Universe

The 707 Freedom Series

Free

Freeing Jasper

Finally Free

Freedom

The Next Generation (707 spinoff)

Saving Meadow

Chasing Honor

ACKNOWLEDGMENTS

First and foremost, I need to thank my fellow Collective authors—Chris Genovese, Ellie Masters, Erin Trejo, Elias Raven, and Carver Pike. I cannot begin to express how honored I am to collaborate with such a great group of authors. I've had so much fun plotting and planning this series with them. They all have taught me so much, and I could not be more grateful.

Chris Genovese, my brother, thank you for always being my sounding board. You are by and far the most creative person I know. Your imagination knows no bounds. It is a beautiful thing to watch your brain work.

Ellie Masters, as always, you pushed me to finish this book. Our word sprints and you reveling when you beat me always pushed me to do better. You have been instrumental in my progression as a writer. Knowing that you will be reading my words and critiquing them is both terrifying and yet comforting. You make me a better writer. Thank you for everything.

Erin Trejo, I was a huge fan of your work long before I ever wrote a single word on a page. You are a mentor, a great friend, and a talented author. It has been so much fun working with you.

Elias Raven, you friend, are a force of nature. You are the tornado that blows through, and all you can do is pray your grip is strong enough to hold on. I have said it a thousand times before, but it bears repeating, you are an outstanding writer. You cross genres, eras, and writing styles with ease. I am so thankful to have had a chance to work with you.

Carver Pike, I can only thank you for the many sleepless nights. 'Who knew scary could be so sexy?'

The Collective is so blessed to have a huge support team behind us! Thank you to all the BETA readers and reviewers that gave us feedback. It undoubtedly made this series better. We cannot thank you enough for your time, hard work, and dedication to this project.

The Collective PA and Overlord Michelle Thomas, thank you doesn't begin to cover what we all owe you. You have five authors to keep straight, five authors to wrangle, five authors to promote. It is a wonder how you pull it all off. Thank you.

Thank you to all of my readers! You are, as always,

the reason I do this. The reason I stay up until the wee hours of the morning. The reason I agonize over each and every word I type. The reason I pull my hair out during editing. The reason I love what I do. The reason I get to be who I've always wanted to be. XOXO—Riley

ABOUT THE AUTHOR

Riley Edwards is a bestselling multi-genre author, wife, and military mom. Riley was born and raised in Los Angeles but now resides on the east coast with her fantastic husband and children.

Riley writes heart-stopping romance with sexy alpha heroes and even stronger heroines. Riley's favorite genres to write are romantic suspense and military romance.

Don't forget to sign up for Riley's newsletter and never miss another release, sale, or exclusive bonus material. https://www.subscribepage.com/RRsignup

Facebook Fan Group

www.rileyedwardsromance.com

facebook.com/Novelist.Riley.Edwards

twitter.com/rileyedwardsrom

instagram.com/rileyedwardsromance

bookbub.com/authors/riley-edwards

amazon.com/author/rileyedwards

Made in the USA
Monee, IL
20 January 2020

20577353R00174